Abby had a sick feeling.

Maybe sensing her discomfort, Noah stepped closer. "I'm not leaving your side, Abby. Not until we find out what's going on."

She took a deep breath. "I appreciate everything you've done, but I have my dog and my gun. I want you to leave." Her heart was pounding. She needed time to process the information he'd unearthed about her parents.

With a locked jaw, he stood. "Fine." That was all he said before he walked out.

Quickly packing a bag, she called Bates to her side and locked the door behind them. She needed to talk to Grammy. She had the sinking feeling her grandmother knew more about her parents than she let on.

She opened the car door when she spotted something on the seat. The dog released a low growl when Abby tensed, staring at the item in horror. It couldn't be...

In shock, she backed away. Her life was spinning out of control and nobody could stop the madness.

Betrayed Birthright is **Liz Shoaf**'s first published inspirational novel. She's been writing for many years, and hopes this is the beginning of a long and fulfilling career. When not writing or training her dogs for agility trials, Liz enjoys spending time with family, jogging and singing in the choir at church whenever possible. To find out more about Liz, you can visit and contact her through her website, www.lizshoaf.com, or email her at phelpsliz1@gmail.com.

Books by Liz Shoaf

Love Inspired Suspense

Betrayed Birthright

BETRAYED BIRTHRIGHT

LIZ SHOAF

HARLEQUIN® LOVE INSPIRED® SUSPENSE

Recycling programs
for this product may
not exist in your area.

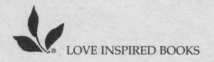

LOVE INSPIRED BOOKS

ISBN-13: 978-0-373-45733-5

Betrayed Birthright

Copyright © 2017 by Liz Phelps

Printed in U.S.A.

For even your brothers and the household of your father,
even they have dealt treacherously with you,
even they have cried aloud after you do not believe them,
although they may say nice things to you.
–Jeremiah 12:6

A special note to my dad, Reverend Kermit E. Shoaf, from your baby girl. You armed me with faith and courage to face whatever comes my way, and I thank you for that. I miss you and can't wait to see you again when my time is at hand.

To my editor, Dina Davis, and her boss, for taking a chance on a newbie. And a special shout-out to all the various departments at Harlequin who work so hard to make dreams come true.

ONE

Abigail Mayfield gripped the covers, fear icing the breath in her throat as she strained to hear the noise again. A slight sound had disturbed her sleep. She closed her eyes against the darkness and listened intently. An unnatural silence greeted her. The wind was calm and no tree branches brushed against the side of the house because she'd had them removed after buying the property.

Her eyes blinked open when she heard a small scratching sound. *The stalker is here!* She had moved all the way across the country for nothing. She struggled to breathe and goose bumps pimpled her arms until a cold, wet nose nudged her neck.

In slow increments, Abby forced herself to relax and silently thanked her grandmother for helping her find a trained protection dog before she moved to Texas.

"Bates," she whispered, "did you hear that noise, boy?"

The seventy-pound, playful but dead-serious-about-his-job, black-and-tan Belgian Malinois grabbed her blanket with his teeth and tugged it off the bed. That was answer enough.

As quietly as possible, she slid out of bed, grabbed her

cell phone off the nightstand, along with the Glock 19 pistol her grandmother had given her last year for Christmas. She might appear to be a harmless Tinker Bell—and had been called that on occasion—but appearances were deceiving. While growing up, her grandmother made sure she knew how to handle a gun.

"God, I need a little help here," she whispered as they moved toward the bedroom door. The dog glued to her side bolstered her confidence. Bates would attack an assailant, but his main job was to protect her; at least, that's what the trainer had said during the handler classes.

Tinkling glass hit the kitchen tile floor and left no doubt that someone was breaking and entering. At the top of the stairs, Abby took a deep, steadying breath. She buried her fear—the way Daddy had taught her—dialed 911 with one hand and held the pistol loosely at her side with the other. She had the advantage at the top of the stairs. If someone tried to come up, she'd fire a warning shot.

"Nine-one-one. Is this an emergency?"

Having turned the volume down before leaving the bedroom, Abby held the phone close to her ear. "This is Abby Mayfield. Someone is breaking into my house," she whispered.

"Ma'am, leave your phone on and keep it with you. We can track you through your cell if circumstances change, but for now, give me your address."

Abby swallowed hard. She knew what that meant. They could track her if the assailant removed her from the house. "My address is 135 Grove Street, Blessing, Texas."

"Stay hidden if you can. We'll have a squad car there as soon as possible."

Abby didn't respond because the sound of soft footsteps climbing the wooden stairs reached her ears. This scenario was the reason she'd removed all the carpet and installed wood and tile floors. She raised the Glock and Bates released a low, snarling growl. Bless his heart. The sweet animal she knew and loved sounded as if he wanted to rip someone's throat out, and he probably would if it came down to it.

The footsteps stopped and Abby sensed the menace and hatred floating up the stairs in a thick wave of dark emotion. Whoever it was meant her harm. But why? Who disliked her that much? The police in North Carolina had asked her that question and she still had no answer.

A siren wailed in the distance. Quick footsteps raced back down the stairs and out the kitchen door. Her legs wobbled. Abby plopped onto the top step and blew out a relieved breath. Her dog licked her face and she hugged him close. "Thanks for the help, Bates. I know you'd probably be happier as a police dog, but I sure am glad you're with me."

The trembling in her body started small, but gained momentum as the police cruiser swerving into her driveway illuminated the front of her house.

Noah Galloway pried his eyelids open and squinted at his wristwatch—it was 3:15 a.m.—when his cell phone belted out "God Bless America," his call tune for dispatch. He came fully alert within seconds. "Galloway."

"Sheriff. We have a B and E in progress at 135 Grove Street. Nine-one-one transferred the call."

Night calls were rare. B and Es, even more so in their small town. Grabbing his jeans, he dressed with one hand and held the phone to his ear. "You on your way over?"

"Yes, sir. I'm in my car right now. I'll be there in three minutes. Don't you worry none. I'll take care of Dylan while you're on duty."

He thanked Peggy Sue—his dispatch officer and dedicated babysitter—shoved his gun into his holster, threw on a jacket and raced down the hall. Stepping quietly into his son's room, he reassured himself that Dylan was safely tucked in bed and left the door cracked on his way out.

Peggy Sue was climbing the steps to the front porch as he opened the door.

"Isn't that the address for the church's new choir director?" It was a small town, and as sheriff, he made it his business to keep tabs on everything going on.

"Yes, sir. I can't imagine anyone breaking into a choir director's home. It's blasphemous, is what I think."

Noah ignored the small talk. "Is Cooper on his way?"

"Yep, I called Coop first. Y'all should arrive there about the same time."

Before hopping into his car, he glanced back at Peggy Sue, an older woman who had taken him and Dylan under her wing when they moved to town.

She grinned. "Don't worry. I'll hold down the fort."

Noah gave a curt nod and ducked his head as he folded his long frame into the squad car. He estimated he'd arrive at the scene within five minutes. Grove Street was located on the outskirts of town, where quite a few older homes had been built during the town's more prosperous days.

His jaw clenched when he turned a street corner. Coop had flipped on his siren, and red and blue lights were streaming through the neighborhood. *Nothing like alerting the perpetrator to our presence.* Taking a deep breath for patience, he exited his patrol car just as his young, energetic deputy flung his car door open and presented himself as a target.

Noah motioned Cooper to the back of his squad car and reminded himself that his deputy was new at the job. The eagerness shining out of Cooper's eyes reminded Noah of himself many years ago, before disillusionment set in.

Before he had a chance to put his plans into motion, a woman came careening down the front porch steps. He gauged her to be about five foot three, a little over a hundred pounds with long, soft-looking blond hair. Her eyes were rounded and her mouth formed a grim line. Dressed in pajamas decorated with big pink hearts, she yelled while pointing toward the side of the house.

"He fled through the kitchen door when he heard your sirens. You'll have to hurry if you want to catch him." Her breath came out in short gasps.

Noah nodded at his deputy. "Go ahead, Coop."

"Yes, sir." Coop gave a crisp salute.

He doubted the perpetrator was still in the area—the only reason Noah allowed Cooper to go after him. Keeping a close eye on the dog that had accompanied the woman outside—and the pistol that looked much too comfortable in her hand for his peace of mind—Noah made a closer assessment of the woman shivering in front of him. He estimated her to be in her midtwenties and her eyes were dark brown. Peering deep into those eyes, he recognized courage overlapping the fear.

He shook off those fanciful thoughts. Though he'd heard the church had hired a new choir director, they'd never met. "Sheriff Galloway, ma'am. Maybe we should take this inside. The perpetrator has likely fled, but we don't know that for sure."

She glanced around, as if coming out of shock. The neighbors' lights had started blinking on and he knew people would soon be in the street demanding to know what was happening.

"Where are my manners? Yes. Please come in."

Thinking she might be a little shaky from the ordeal, Noah placed his hand on her elbow but immediately released her when the dog gave a low warning growl. The animal's posture and demeanor indicated intensive training. This wasn't just a pet. The animal looked like a Belgian Malinois, a dog widely used by both the military and police. It sported a short, light brown coat and black covered its face. *And why does a church choir director need a trained attack dog?*

"Control your dog, ma'am, and please hand me the pistol."

She blushed and he couldn't help but notice that the pink in her cheeks matched the hearts on her pajamas.

"I'm so sorry. Bates is a little protective," she said, but after a moment she straightened her shoulders and looked him in the eye with a glint of determination. "No, I'm not sorry. My dog did his job tonight. He protected me."

His second impression of the woman reminded him of a soft Southern belle with some feistiness thrown in. Interesting combination. Noah glanced between the woman and the animal. "I take it he's trained. Give him the release command and he'll back off."

The petite woman faced her dog. "Time to be nice, Bates, baby. Sheriff Galloway is a friend."

His incredulity at her choice of command must have shown on his face when she turned around. Hands propped on her tiny waist, she lifted her chin a notch. "What?"

He swallowed an appalled retort. "Nothing." He would have used a more common "off" or "back" command, but that was her business.

He glanced at the front door. "We should go inside. Let me make sure the house is clear."

She dutifully handed him her weapon. "I have a concealed-carry permit." She sounded as if she was just waiting for him to ask to see it. When he stayed silent, she gave him a sweet, tentative smile, and his protective instincts flared to life.

"And there's no need to check the house. Bates would alert me if even a mouse dared to invade his territory."

"That may be true, but I still need to check the point of entry."

The dog had disappeared, but met them when they stepped into the house and moved to the kitchen through which she claimed the assailant had fled. Based on the broken glass pane, it was obvious how the intruder had entered the premises. The ground outside was dry and there were only slight impressions of shoes on the grass. Not enough for a print.

"That windowpane will have to be replaced and you need a dead bolt on this door."

"I'll take care of it tomorrow."

The window would be repaired before he left, but for the moment, he nodded and she led the way to the living room. Outside, the house reflected a Victorian style, and this room was decorated in the same theme. Shelves filled with picture frames lined one wall. They contained photos of children of all ages. A beautiful black, antique-looking baby grand piano was show-cased in the room.

As she sat down on a love seat, she smiled and stared, a fond look on her face, at the photographs. "Those are past and present students. I teach piano lessons in my spare time. I'm also the choir director at the local—the only—church in Blessing."

He sat on the couch across from her and stifled his protective urges. He knew nothing about this woman. She had moved to Blessing eight months ago, but he hadn't been to church since his wife died two years earlier.

"Ma'am, describe the break-in. Anything you can remember." She looked so innocent sitting there, her feet tucked under her and her shoulder-length hair slightly mussed. But he knew looks could be deceiving. He'd learned that during his five-year tenure with the FBI before moving back to Blessing to run for sheriff.

"I haven't introduced myself. My name is Abby Mayfield."

Surprisingly, she was very detailed in her account of events. Almost as if she she'd done this before. Suspicious now, he asked the normal questions, but his gut screamed that there was much more to Abby Mayfield than met the eye.

"Do you keep valuables in the house? Anything that might tempt a burglar?" Statistics showed that most thieves broke into empty homes when people were out of town. Not when they were asleep in bed. The perpetrator had a bigger chance of getting caught if people were in the house.

Fiddling with a string on the bottom of her pajama top, she bit her lip, as if debating how much to tell. Noah leaned forward, placing his elbows on his thighs. "Ms. Mayfield—Abby—I can't help you if you don't come clean with me."

Her chin notched up and he was momentarily pulled into the deep pools of her dark brown eyes. He pulled back, refusing to go there. He had responsibilities now. A motherless, six-year-old son. Ms. Mayfield might appear as harmless as a newly unfurled flower, but he reminded himself again that looks could be deceiving.

The dog settled at her feet, placing himself solidly between the two of them. She leaned down and rubbed his head.

"I guess I have to trust someone and you look dependable enough."

He kept his expression all business when she lifted her eyes, as if she was assessing his trustworthiness.

Releasing a sigh, she sat up straight. "I moved to Blessing, Texas, eight months ago because there were several incidents where I lived in North Carolina." He didn't miss the slight tremor in her voice. "There were two break-ins at my home, but praise the Lord, I had a high-quality alarm system. There was also—" she placed her hand on the dog's head again, as if for reassurance "—a car that I'm pretty sure tried to run me down, but nothing that could be proven."

Noah made notes on the pad he had pulled out of his shirt pocket. "Did you report the incidents to the local police?"

She nodded. "I sure did. They were very nice and did a thorough investigation. They questioned my co-workers at church, along with all my music students' parents. They found nothing." Her expression turned quizzical. "It's the craziest thing ever. I don't have one enemy that I know of, and it's not as if I own anything valuable. I'm a choir director and piano teacher. I can't imagine anyone wanting to hurt me."

The exasperation in her voice almost made him smile. She was a cute wisp of air.

"During the investigation, did they delve into your family background?"

If anything, she became even more vexed. "There's only me and my grandmother. My parents died in a car accident when I was six. They were both only children. Grammy is the only family I have left. She's still in North Carolina. I'm trying to encourage her to move here, but I'm not sure what to do now. Whoever did those terrible things in North Carolina has apparently followed me to Texas."

She shuddered and Noah had the sudden urge to take this petite woman home with him where he could protect her and keep her safe. Ignoring his thoughts, he scribbled in his notebook.

"Have you received any threatening letters or phone calls?"

"No, nothing."

"Is that why you moved to Blessing? Because of the danger?"

"Yes, and because I didn't want my grandmother to get hurt. She lived three houses down from me. The police didn't even have a lead, and now this mess has followed me here."

"How did you come to pick Blessing?"

For the first time, a full smile bloomed on her face and his heart lurched. He still missed his wife, but it had been two years since ovarian cancer had claimed her life.

"Grammy got really worried after the second break-in. The police were cruising the neighborhood every once in a while, but it didn't stop the intruders. She hoped whoever was after me was local and would leave me alone if I moved across the country. We studied a map of Texas and she decided that Blessing, with a population of 967, would be a good place to move. It would be hard for the person after me to hide in such a small town."

She leaned forward and grinned. "Did you know Blessing was founded in 1903? The leaders of the town changed the original name from *Thank God* to *Blessing* after the United States Postal Service rejected the first name and refused to deliver the mail. Isn't that a hoot?"

Noah noted that Abby had a sweet, bubbly personality.

"Interesting piece of information. I grew up here and never heard that story. I'll have to share it with my son. Is this the first incident that's happened since you arrived in Blessing?"

Her smile slipped away, and he missed the warmth of it, but they had an intruder to catch and catch them he would. He was a tenacious investigator, if the *media* was to be believed. He may have left the FBI to run for sheriff in his hometown, but his instincts ran true. And if he admitted the truth, he was ready to sink his teeth into something more than lost dogs and domestic disputes.

He would do everything in his power to keep Abby Mayfield safe.

TWO

Abby studied Sheriff Galloway. He looked familiar, but she couldn't place him. The break-in had done a number on her. She'd really believed she'd left whoever was trying to harm her behind in North Carolina. She could still hardly believe anyone hated her enough to try to run her down with a car or break into her house.

But what could a small-town Texas sheriff do that the authorities in North Carolina hadn't been able to accomplish? Remnants of a newspaper article floated through her mind, and then it hit her. "You're that famous FBI guy from New York." Her heart beat faster. "You rooted out those mafia guys trying to kill the mayor and saved his life. It was all over the news."

Sheriff Galloway surely stood over six feet and sported short, dark hair. He was a handsome man, in a rugged sort of way, but when those electric-blue eyes focused intently on her, memories of the newscasts filtered through her mind.

"I'm sorry about your wife." It had been reported that his wife passed away, but at least he still had his son. She had lost her precious unborn baby boy after receiving news of her husband's death several years earlier.

He glanced down at his notebook. "Thank you."

For the first time since the whole mess started, Abby felt a stirring of hope. "Do you think you can find out who's doing this to me?"

He raised his head. A steely glint filled his eyes. "I'll do my best."

Abby sensed a fierce determination. Once he'd picked up the trail of an enemy, he would never stop. He seemed trustworthy, but she wouldn't care to be on the bad side of this particular lawman. His hunting instincts shone bright from his eyes. She privately pegged him as a good predator hunting very dangerous parasites.

"One more question."

"Yes?"

"Are there any irate husbands or boyfriends in the picture I need to know about?"

Sadness engulfed her as she thought of John, her dear sweet husband, gone on to be with the Lord. "No. My husband died three years ago and I haven't dated since."

"Any problems with the in-laws?"

"No. They're nice people, but I'm sad to say we kind of drifted apart after John's death."

"Ma'am—"

"Please, call me Abby."

"Abby. Is there anyone you can call to come stay with you for what's left of the night?"

She shook her head. "There are people at the church I attend who would be more than willing to come, but I'll never be able to go back to sleep, and I have Bates. He'll alert me if anyone comes back." She pointed at her Glock where he'd laid it on a side table. "I know how to use that, and I won't hesitate if someone comes after me."

The right side of his mouth kicked up in a slight grin.

"I don't doubt that at all."

Heat warmed her face. "When I was younger, my grandmother taught me to shoot. She was of the opinion that any self-respecting Southern lady should know how to handle a gun. I practice every once in a while to keep my aim good."

"I'm sure that's true, but I can't leave you alone until the broken windowpane is fixed and the house is secure."

He was going to stay here? Abby needed time to assimilate everything that had happened and calm down. She needed some time to herself.

"That's not necessary, I'll be fine."

"I'll wait outside in the squad car until the hardware store opens. I'll make sure someone comes out first thing to fix the glass."

Abby felt bad, thinking of him sitting outside alone in his car, but not enough to ask him to stay inside with her until the sun came up.

She accompanied him to the front door and turned the dead bolt after he left. Rushing to the living room window, which fronted the house, she watched as he conferred with his deputy, who'd been waiting by his car. After a few minutes, the deputy drove away and the sheriff settled inside his car, hunkered down for what was left of the night.

The house quieted and loneliness shrouded her. After a few minutes, she turned toward the kitchen. A strong cup of coffee would lift her spirits.

Crossing the threshold of the warm, homey room, she glanced out the window over the kitchen sink, stared at the cruiser and thought about Sheriff Galloway staying there to protect her. She got a warm, fuzzy feeling until she glanced up and to the left, and spotted something that shouldn't be there. Her smile disappeared and fear sank its vicious teeth into her belly, worked its way to her throat—almost strangling her with its intensity.

Even with the town's limited resources, Noah refused to leave Ms. Mayfield with no protection. He'd handle it off the clock. He lowered the car window and called Peggy Sue. After checking that everything was safe on the home front and confirming his dispatcher could stay the rest of the night with Dylan, Noah stiffened when he spotted Ms. Mayfield running out the front door, waving both hands in his direction.

He left the car door open as he burst out of the vehicle, his Smith & Wesson M&P9 9 mm pistol in hand. The gun felt comfortable, an extension of his arm. He met her at the end of the sidewalk.

"What's wrong?"

The blood had drained from her face, but she took a deep breath and composed herself. He was impressed. She had a lot of courage packed into her small frame.

"There's something inside that shouldn't be there."

Before addressing her concern, he followed procedure. "Are you sure no one is in the house?"

She began to speak, but stopped, her expression uncertain.

Noah glanced at the dog. He was glued to Abby's side. "Let me clear the house and then you can show me what you found."

She gave a brisk nod.

It didn't take long to check the house and Noah went back outside. "Let's go in."

She followed him into the kitchen, took a deep breath and pointed at a cabinet built into the wall above the counter. "That's a picture of my mom and dad, but I've never seen it before."

Noah grabbed a paper towel, opened the glass-fronted cabinet door and removed the picture, placing it on the kitchen island in the center of the room. He studied the photograph. Her parents were standing on a beach with nothing but ocean behind them, no identifying landmarks to be found. He focused on the couple. Abby's father was a handsome man, her mother pretty and petite, same as her daughter. A smiling child was held in the father's arms. All wore big smiles. Life looked perfect.

"Are you sure you've never seen this before?"

She rubbed her arms. "I'm positive. I've never seen the photograph or the frame. I've seen plenty of pictures of my parents, but none of them were taken on a beach."

The phone on the wall awoke with a high shrill and Abby jumped. Noah held his hand up when she took a step forward. "Let me answer it."

She nodded.

"Sheriff Galloway."

A moment of silence filled the phone line before a strong voice almost shattered his eardrum. "What's a sheriff doing at my granddaughter's house at five thirty in the morning?" The woman didn't give him a chance to answer. "I woke up a little while ago and felt the urge to start praying. You listen, and you listen good. I want to speak to Abby this minute."

If the situation hadn't been so serious, Noah would have grinned at the older woman's audacity. Abby crossed the room and Noah was glad to see her eyes shining with laughter instead of concern.

"Sorry about that. It's my grandmother. I heard her clear across the room."

Noah handed Abby the phone and she started talking. "Grammy? No, ma'am, everything is fine. There's been a break-in, but Sheriff Galloway is here. I'll explain everything in the morning…Yes, Baby Bates did his job well and I have my pistol. I keep it on the nightstand right beside the bed." She sighed. "Yes, I do believe it's connected to what happened in North Carolina. I'll call you tomorrow after we know more, but, Grammy, please be careful."

Noah's ears pricked when Abby turned away from him and lowered her voice. "Grammy! That's not important. Fine, yes, he's good-looking. Now, go back to bed and stop worrying. Everything is fine."

Noah cleared his throat, buried his grin and busied himself by looking at the photo again as she hung up the phone. She swung around and her face had turned that sweet shade of pink he was coming to adore.

"That was my grandmother."

They both knew he was already aware of that and the pink turned a shade darker.

Noah briefly wondered what it would be like to have a grandparent who loved you enough to call at five thirty in the morning to check on you. His grandfather loved him, but the crusty old man wasn't exactly what you'd call cuddly. He almost grinned at the thought, but cleared his throat instead.

"I'll have Deputy Cooper dust the picture frame and the break-in area for prints tomorrow."

Bates moved into position beside Abby. Noah had always wished to be a K-9 handler, but his position in the FBI hadn't warranted it. He'd heard a lot about the Belgian Malinois breed. Alert, ready for action and easy to train.

"Why don't you try to get some sleep? I'll stay the rest of the night in the squad car and keep watch."

She nodded, but then stopped. "I won't be able to sleep. Why don't I get dressed and make us some breakfast?"

Her offer was better than sitting in the patrol car. "Sounds good."

Abby beat a hasty retreat upstairs. She had been more shaken than she had let on. Deep down, the terror still reigned. She couldn't believe this mess had followed her all the way to Texas. She wanted her grandmother, but wouldn't dare move Grammy here until the situation was resolved.

She pulled pants and a sweater from an antique wooden wardrobe, shed her pajamas and dressed. In the bathroom, she glanced in the mirror and groaned. "My hair looks like a rat's nest." Not that it mattered under the circumstances, but Sheriff Galloway was a sharp-looking man. She smiled, thinking about her grandmother's antics. The older woman was forever nudging Abby back into the dating game.

She brushed her teeth and tamed her hair before hurrying back downstairs, only to realize Bates wasn't dogging her heels. Stepping into the kitchen, she saw why. Noah had started the coffee and was rooting around in the refrigerator with Bates glued to his side. The dog was definitely food driven, just like the trainer had said.

"You've stolen my baby boy's affection."

Noah jumped and hit his head on the rack above him. Abby rushed forward. "I'm so sorry. I didn't mean to startle you."

Noah glared at Bates. "Some guard dog you are."

Laughter bubbled up and it felt good. "He does love

his food. The trainer told me to keep him on a strict diet, but I slip him a few goodies now and then."

Rubbing his head, Noah straightened and froze when he looked at her.

Her hand reached for her hair. "What? Is my hair sticking out?"

The right side of his mouth kicked up and her heart pattered.

"No, it's just… Never mind."

An awkward silence filled the room and Abby practically ran to the refrigerator. "We can have eggs, toast and coffee if that's okay."

He nodded and took a seat on one of the bar stools.

"How do you like your eggs?"

"I'm not picky. Whatever is easy."

Eventually an easy camaraderie filled the room while she cooked their simple meal. She remembered spending many mornings similar to this one with John. The memory filled her with mixed emotions.

Loading the food on the plates, she placed them on the kitchen island counter, took a seat across from him and bent her head to pray. "Lord, bless this food we're about to eat. Keep us safe and help us solve the mystery surrounding me. Amen."

"Amen." Noah picked up his fork and began eating. "We'll start by making a list of possible suspects."

Abby chewed and swallowed. "But there are no suspects. That's what I keep telling everyone. And I have students coming for piano lessons today."

"We'll work around that."

A terrible thought crossed her mind. "Are my students safe coming here after what happened?"

His jaw turned to granite and those electric-blue eyes

hardened. "We'll keep you and your students safe, Ms. Mayfield."

Warmth and a sense of well-being filled her. She believed him. "Thank you, and please call me Abby."

They finished eating their meal in silence. Abby glanced at the photograph still sitting on the opposite end of the kitchen island. Her hand, holding a forkful of scrambled eggs, froze halfway to her mouth.

Noah straightened in his chair and his gaze sharpened. "What is it?"

She didn't want the photo anywhere near her, but she had to be sure. Laying her fork aside, she stood and slowly walked around the island. Chills snaked up her spine as she leaned over and studied the picture of the happy couple holding a laughing child.

Almost a living thing, dread crept into the very core of her being. "The child in the picture? It isn't me."

THREE

The call of the investigative hunt pulsated through Noah's veins. Every instinct screamed this was a major missing piece of the puzzle, but Abby's obvious devastation shook him to the core. His first impulse was to comfort her. He wanted to promise he would make this situation go away, but that wasn't going to happen. They needed answers.

Maybe trying to find solutions to her problems would calm her down. He pulled out a notepad and pen, making it routine. "You're certain you've never seen the photo before?"

Sliding into a chair across from him, she stared at the picture a moment, then jerked her gaze back to his. "I've never seen that picture in my life."

"And the child? You don't recognize the child?"

She slowly shook her head. "No. I'm an only child and I don't have any cousins." Her eyes brightened. "You know what? The boy in that picture looks to be about a year old. I bet this was taken before I was born and my dad is holding a friend's child. Maybe my parents went to the beach with another couple."

Noah's gut told him otherwise, but he needed more information, so he kept his opinions to himself. "Let's begin by writing down the names of any new people in your life."

"I can't think of anyone who would want to hurt me." Her voice rose in anger and frustration. "I love living in Blessing, and after so many months passing with no more incidents, I was convinced I'd left this mess behind in North Carolina. I was ready to bring Grammy to Blessing, but this dangerous situation has to be resolved first."

Noah lifted a brow. Abby's back straightened and her shoulders squared. The steel had overridden the putty, and the transformation was amazing. Determination lit her eyes. Abby would be a fantastic mother—deep down, he knew she would fiercely protect a child of her own. He pushed that crazy, unprofessional thought aside and returned to the important issue at hand.

"You said you moved to Blessing eight months ago. Besides the permanent residents in town, have any new people entered your life? Choir members, music students?"

She placed her elbows on the table and leaned forward. "I'm fairly new to town, so everyone is new to me, but all of my piano students are from Blessing. The only new people I can think of are two that recently joined the choir, but surely they didn't have anything to do with the break-in."

Noah raised a brow. "Their names?"

"Joanne Ferguson and Walter Fleming. They're both nice people. She's been here about four months and he joined a couple of weeks ago. He's the best tenor I've ever worked with."

Noah almost smiled. Abby was such an innocent. "So, because he has a great voice, he can't be a bad person?"

Her lips puckered and he choked back a laugh. He hadn't laughed much in a long time. Not since his wife died, and especially not after the threats against his son's life in retaliation for Noah killing Anthony Vitale's father, Big Jack. Both men had been involved in the attempt on the mayor's life in New York, but they were only able to find evidence on the mafia father. Noah had his own reasons for living in Blessing.

"That's not what I said." She popped out the words, then took a deep breath. "I apologize. Please, go on, but we have to hurry. I have students coming."

"Aren't they in school?"

"Yes. Normally I give lessons later in the afternoon, but we have a recital coming up and the principal allowed them to miss a few classes so we can get in some extra practice. There's an advantage to living in a small town."

Abby's enthusiasm was contagious and Noah's spirits lifted. "I'll hurry it along. We should delve into your background," he said. "Your parents died when you were six years old?"

"Yes. They were on vacation in Jackson Hole, Wyoming, and both died in a car crash. The police deemed it an accident. Neither one had any siblings. My dad's parents passed away when he was in his twenties, and Grammy is my only living relative."

"Where were your parents born and raised?"

Exasperation filled her voice. "What does that have to do with the break-in?"

"Humor me."

"Fine. They were born and grew up in Mocksville, North Carolina. It's a small town located between Charlotte and Winston-Salem."

"Their names?" Her lips puckered again and Noah

hid a smile. They'd only known each other a few hours and already he could read some of her expressions. The pucker equaled irritation.

"Lee and Mary Beauchamp."

He dutifully wrote down their names. First, he'd do surface searches on Joanne Ferguson and Walter Fleming. If he had any trouble, he'd connect with a few of his old FBI buddies. As far as her parents were concerned, if they grew up and stayed in North Carolina, it shouldn't be hard to find information. "Okay, this is enough to get me started. I'll have Cooper bring my laptop when he comes to dust for prints so I can get to work on this."

When she didn't respond, Noah glanced up. Her lips were pursed.

"So you meant what you said, you're staying until the glass pane is repaired? You don't have to do that. I'll be perfectly fine here with Bates, and as I said, I am proficient with a gun in a worst-case scenario. Surely whoever broke in won't return in broad daylight."

"Ms. Mayfield, I won't leave until I'm convinced you're safe." His tone left no room for argument.

She gave him a mischievous grin. "Fine, but don't say I didn't warn you. Listening to beginner music students is not for the faint of heart."

If she was trying to get rid of him, it wasn't working. "I'll take my chances."

A car horn blared outside and Noah jumped to his feet, one hand automatically reaching for the gun in his side holster.

"Settle down, cowboy, that's probably Trevor, here for his piano lesson." He glared at her, but her eyes twinkled as she moved toward the foyer.

He bolted in front of her and reached the door first. Her brows rose in question and he cleared his throat, feeling like a rookie. He didn't like the sentiment. "I'll go first and make sure the front yard is clear."

She chuckled and he opened the door and they stepped out. A white SUV sat idling at the curb. Noah recognized Mrs. Johnson's vehicle. Her son, Trevor—with whom Noah was well acquainted—threw open the passenger door and shuffled up the sidewalk with hunched shoulders. His eyes rounded when he spotted Noah standing beside Abby.

Stopping on the bottom step, his head whipped back and forth between the adults.

"You in trouble with the law, Ms. Mayfield?" he asked, his voice filled with something akin to admiration.

Amused, Noah waited to see how Abby would respond. She patted her hair down and released a nervous laugh. "Trevor, you know better than that. Sheriff Galloway just stopped by to check on me."

Trevor moved up the steps, patted her arm and gave Noah a sly grin. "It's okay, Ms. Mayfield, I won't tell anybody the sheriff was at your house first thing in the morning. That is, if you can find it in your heart to let me skip piano lessons today."

Abby's mouth fell open, then snapped shut. "Trevor Johnson, I can't believe you just tried to blackmail me. Sheriff Galloway has a very good reason for being here, and it's none of your business." She pointed a finger at the front door. "Now, march right into the living room and prepare for your lesson."

Trevor's shoulders slumped as he slowly trudged into the house.

Abby's cheeks were pink with frustration and Noah's mouth stretched into a wide grin. "The kid's a terror. A few weeks ago I had him doing community service—picking up trash—for a minor infraction."

She waved a hand through the air and talked fast. "I don't want to know what that boy's been up to. I better get inside before he destroys my house."

Noah laughed out loud and it felt amazing. He gave her a small salute. "I'm sure you can handle it."

The woman disappeared into the house, and Noah scanned the front yard while pulling his smartphone out of his pocket. He typed a text instructing Cooper to bring his laptop to Ms. Mayfield's house and added a note to swing by his house and pick him up a change of clothes, but then he changed his mind and cleared the text. Instead, he told Cooper to come to Ms. Mayfield's and plan to stay for an hour or so. He'd go home, take a shower, make sure things were well on the home front and pick up his laptop. Cooper texted back and said he was on his way.

Noah slid his phone back into his pocket and checked the surrounding area again. He wouldn't have insisted on staying close to Ms. Mayfield if the break-in had been a normal grab and run. His intuition—one that had served him well during his tenure at the FBI—was screaming that trouble had followed her from North Carolina and the situation was more complicated than either of them imagined.

Hearing mangled piano notes filter out the front door, he opted to stay outside and sat down on the porch swing to await the arrival of his deputy. He pulled his phone out again. He'd check in with his grandfather, Houston, and make sure he was available to take care of Dylan in case Noah found himself tied up longer than expected.

For the first time in a long while, he was excited

about work. Moving to Blessing had been the right thing to do, but truth be told, he missed being in the FBI. The big cases. The camaraderie between agents. He missed it all, but Dylan was safe in Blessing, and his son was the most important thing in his life.

Abby waved at Mrs. Johnson as she picked up Trevor after his piano lesson. Going back inside the house, she closed the door and released a deep sigh. Her dog sat on the floor, his eyes tracking every move she made. "Mercy, Bates. That was a long hour. That child is a terror. As much as I'd love to have a houseful of children, I think I might pass if I thought I'd get one like Trevor."

Bates canted his head to the side and Abby chuckled. "I know. We take what God grants us, and we're to be happy about it, but I'm still going to say a prayer for Mrs. Johnson. She's been blessed with such a… unique child."

Abby glanced around the foyer. She rubbed both arms as the previous night flashed through her mind. She still couldn't believe whoever was after her in North Carolina had followed her to Texas. She hadn't tried to hide or cover her tracks. She and Grammy had hoped it was someone local to North Carolina and the move would get rid of the problem. The worst part of the situation was that Abby couldn't think of a soul who would do something like this to her.

The police in North Carolina had interviewed everyone she knew and come up empty. The entire thing was scary and frustrating. She headed into the kitchen and gave Deputy Cooper a curt nod. He had a pained expression on his face as he took a sip of coffee, no doubt from Trevor's less-than-sterling piano skills, but she didn't feel sorry for him. He had opted to sit out the piano lesson in the relative safety of the kitchen after Noah fled the scene and left his deputy to babysit. The repairman had come, fixed the glass pane and left. She didn't understand why Cooper was still there. As she had learned in North Carolina, the police didn't offer personal bodyguard protection for a mere break-in.

Cooper stuck his nose back into the newspaper in his hands, and she picked up the landline to call her grandmother. She needed to hear a familiar voice.

"Hello."

"Grammy? It's Abby."

"Girl, I've been worried sick. It's about time you called."

Abby closed her eyes as her grandmother's loving voice washed over her. "Sheriff Galloway left his deputy here with me and I had a piano lesson, but everything's fine." The handset was wireless and she stepped into the foyer, lowering her voice. "Grammy, you're not going to believe this. Sheriff Galloway is the FBI agent who saved the life of New York's mayor."

Silence.

"Grammy?"

"I remember reading about him in the newspaper. It was a big deal back then. He cut the head off the mafia beast in New York. They still bring it up in the news periodically. Everyone claims he's an ace investigator, that he never gives up or backs down until he has his man. Wonder how he ended up becoming the sheriff in Blessing?"

Uneasiness scaled down Abby's spine. Grammy made an effort to sound normal, but Abby sensed that something was amiss.

"Grammy, is something wrong? Is everything okay?"

A nervous chuckle filled her ear.

"Of course it is."

Maybe Abby was imagining things. "Well, if anything happens, call me immediately."

"Same with you, sweetie. I better go now. The bridge group is meeting for lunch."

"Okay. And, Grammy?"

"Yes?"

"As soon as this is over, we're moving you to Blessing. My house is large enough for both of us." Her grandmother was fast approaching her mideighties, and Abby had been trying to encourage her to move in with her for several years now. Her grandmother always insisted she needed her own space, but Abby knew the older woman was secretly hoping Abby would start dating and eventually get married and have a house filled with her own family.

"I'm coming to Blessing, but we'll talk about whether I'm moving in with you later."

"Okay. Love you."

"Love you, too."

Feeling better after a shower and change of clothes, and after lining up Grandfather Houston to take care of Dylan in case he was tied up for a few days, Noah knocked on Ms. Mayfield's front door. A warning bark echoed through the house and Noah felt better knowing she had the dog.

But not better enough to leave her alone in the house. He couldn't justify spending city money on personal protection, so he'd called the mayor and taken a week's vacation. Hopefully, Cooper could handle anything that came up at the station.

He didn't examine his motives too closely. Ms. Mayfield was a resident in his jurisdiction and he would do everything in his power to protect her. At least, that's what he told himself.

He grinned when Cooper opened the door with his hand on his holster.

His deputy blew out a deep breath. "I sure am glad to see you, Sheriff."

"Piano lesson that bad, was it?"

His deputy rolled his eyes. "Ms. Mayfield must have a ton of patience."

Itching to get to work, he waved Cooper out the door, onto the front porch. "Listen, I put in for a week's vacation so I can work on Ms. Mayfield's problem. There's more here than a mere break-in. Her life may be in jeopardy. I'm putting you in charge at the station."

Cooper's eyes widened and his chest puffed out. "I won't let you down, sir."

Noah almost chuckled at the eagerness in his deputy's eyes. "I know you'll do your best. Just call me on my cell if something comes up that you can't handle."

Cooper swallowed hard. "Sheriff, I know you think I'm a country bumpkin, and I also know the only reason I got this job is because my daddy is the mayor, but I'm proud to be working alongside someone with your experience. I've already learned a lot from you."

Noah nodded at the gangly twenty-three-year-old staring at him with an earnest expression on his face. "You've come a long way."

Time to get down to business. "You find any prints while dusting?"

Cooper shook his head. "I took Abby's prints for matching, and called in a favor to get the prints run quickly. I ruled out all the smaller prints that would belong to her students—who are all kids—and I didn't find anything else. The intruder must have worn gloves."

The information didn't surprise Noah. From the beginning this case hadn't felt like a routine B and E. "Okay, head back to the station and call if you need me."

"Yes, sir," Cooper said with a big grin on his face.

Noah took a deep breath and opened the door. He had a strong feeling Ms. Mayfield wasn't going to be happy with him dogging her every step.

FOUR

Abby was irritated with Sheriff Galloway for camping out in her home, but deep down, she was also relieved. This whole mess had shaken her more than she cared to admit.

She closed the front door behind her last piano student of the day, turned the dead bolt and grinned as she hurried upstairs to clean up before choir practice. The sheriff had settled himself in the kitchen to work on his laptop, and sound carried well through her historic house. He was probably pulling his hair out by now.

She freshened up in the bathroom and made her way to the kitchen. The sheriff, with Bates lying by his side, glanced up as she sailed through the doorway. "We have just enough time to grab a bite to eat before heading to church." She raised a brow. "I assume you're accompanying me to choir practice?"

Earlier, they'd had a heated discussion about why he needed to hang around, even though secretly she was relieved that he was there while her students were coming and going throughout the afternoon.

He pushed his computer aside and half rose. "What can I do to help?"

Abby opened the refrigerator door. She had to get

dinner on the table. They could talk while they were eating. "Not a thing. We're having leftover lasagna. I'll just stick it in the microwave. It won't take but a few minutes to heat."

The doorbell rang as she put the casserole dish into the microwave and stuck several slices of garlic bread in the oven.

The sheriff scrambled out of his chair and moved in front of her as she headed toward the foyer. "I'll answer the door."

She thought he was being a little overprotective, but bit back a retort and allowed him to answer the door. Standing close behind him, with Bates on her heels, a surprise greeted her as Noah opened the front door. An older gentleman with slightly stooped shoulders gave them a wide grin with a perceptive look in his eyes as he glanced back and forth between Abby and Noah. But most astonishing was the child standing next to him. The boy had to be Noah's son. The youngster was a duplicate of his father, and his interested, electric-blue eyes seemed to be taking her measure.

"My name's Dylan, and you're the choir director at church," he blurted out.

Smiling, Abby made her way around Noah and squatted in front of the boy. "Yes, I surely am, but I haven't had the pleasure of meeting you."

The child shot his father a disgruntled look before turning to her. "Gampy said I had to stay with him because you were having some trouble and needed my dad. Gampy said we came here to offer help in your time of need, and we won't turn down a good meal if it's in the offering." The precocious child lifted his chin. "Dad and Gampy can't cook, and we don't go to church, but a lot of my friends take piano lessons from you and I've seen you around school."

Abby grinned and stood. Dylan was certainly a font of information. "That's right. I come and play the piano when the school is having a special event such as the yearly Christmas play." She grinned. "Which will be coming up soon. As soon as my recitals are finished, we'll start working on the play. You'd make a great Joseph. Why don't you try out for the part?"

His grin revealed a missing front tooth. "Maybe I'll do that."

The older man stuck out his hand. "Name's Houston Galloway." He nodded at Noah. "That's my grandson—" he pointed at Dylan "—and this here's my great-grandson."

Abby shook his hand. "It's nice to meet you, Mr. Galloway."

"I'd be happy for you to call me Houston."

Noah's grandfather and son were a delight. "I'd be happy to call you Houston."

Realizing time was running short, Abby motioned them inside. "Come on in. I have to get to choir practice soon, but we were just about to eat. There's enough lasagna for four if you're hungry."

Two sets of eyes lit up, one young and one old.

Houston spoke for the both of them. "We knew Noah was over here and were hoping you would say that. As Dylan said, us guys don't know our way around the kitchen too much."

Abby ignored Noah's soft snort and led everyone in. Evidently his grandfather was taking care of Dylan while Noah was protecting her.

They moved into the house but came to a standstill in the foyer. Bates stood ready and alert, but his eyes were filled with longing as he gazed at the child. Dylan reflected the same expression.

"A dog," he breathed, awe filling his young voice. "What's his name?"

Abby grinned. A dog and a boy. A match made in heaven. "His name is Bates." She glanced at Sheriff Galloway. "It's fine if they play, but you'll have to give permission."

With wide, excited eyes, Dylan begged his father. "Can I, Dad?"

Sheriff Galloway squatted in front of his son and gently placed a hand on his shoulder. "Bates is a trained attack dog. He's a working animal and you'll have to be careful. You can play with him as long as you're in the same room with us. Now, approach him from the side and squat down beside him so he can sniff you. From a dog's perspective, that's the proper way to greet him."

Abby's heart pinged at the tender way Sheriff Galloway—a hardened former FBI agent—treated his son. A pang of loss gripped her. Her own son, had he lived, would now be over three years old. She stowed away the painful memories and watched as Dylan followed his father's advice. Bates sniffed all around the child and licked his face.

They all laughed and the group moved into the kitchen. "Everyone take a seat. I'll have dinner on the table in a jiff." She laid the table with plates, silverware and napkins, then nuked the whole dish of leftover lasagna and pulled the bread out of the oven. Dylan's eyes rounded when she filled his plate.

"We don't eat like this at home. Dad buys those frozen dinners and sticks them in the microwave."

Abby laughed. "Well, you're having a homemade dinner tonight. When I cook, I always make a lot because I love leftovers." She said grace and everybody dug in. If not for the dangerous incidents that kept happening, Abby would almost feel at peace, but one look into Sheriff Galloway's eyes reminded her that her life would be unsettled until they had some answers.

When they finished eating, Abby stood. "Leave the dishes. I'll clean up after choir practice. I'll be late if I don't hurry."

The sheriff stood. "I'll drive you there."

Houston gave her a peck on the cheek and winked at her, his faded blue eyes twinkling. "That was a mighty fine dinner, Ms. Mayfield. Dylan and I are much obliged. We'll head on and get out of your hair."

Abby gave both of them a hug. "It was my pleasure. Y'all come back soon."

She stood at the door and watched as they walked down the sidewalk and climbed into an old truck.

A throat cleared behind her. "I'm sorry they showed up unannounced. My grandfather tends to live by his own rules."

Abby grinned. "They're quite a pair. I enjoyed both of them."

While waiting for Ms. Mayfield to gather her things, Noah processed the information he'd gathered. Both choir members, Joanne Ferguson and Walter Fleming, had checked out on a surface search. If they didn't find some answers soon, he'd give them a second, deeper look.

Pulling his cell phone out of his pocket, Noah decided to give Sheriff Brady in the Mocksville, North Carolina, police department a quick call to follow up on the previous incidents involving Ms. Mayfield. Maybe Brady had discovered something new.

The phone rang twice before it was answered.

"Mocksville Police Department."

"This is Sheriff Noah Galloway. I'd like to speak with your sheriff."

"Yes, sir. I'll connect you to Sheriff Brady."

"Thank you."

A few seconds passed. "Sheriff Brady speaking."

"I'm Sheriff Galloway, calling from Blessing, Texas. There's been an incident here that involves a former Mocksville resident and I'm gathering information."

A long sigh filled his ear. "I assume you're calling about Abigail Mayfield. I'm aware she moved to Texas about eight months ago. Her grandmother calls me frequently."

After hearing Abby talk to her grandmother on the phone, Noah could imagine the older woman demanding answers.

"What happened this time?" Brady interrupted Noah's musings.

Noah filled him in on the B and E. "She has a trained attack dog and we responded quickly. The intruder fled the premises. No one was hurt, but there is an interesting twist. At some point, someone left a photograph of Ms. Mayfield's parents standing in front of the ocean holding a child. She claims the child isn't her. The picture was placed inside a glass-fronted cabinet in her kitchen. I don't know if the intruder left the picture during the break-in, or if it was left at another time. Ms. Mayfield filled me in on the incidents that happened in your jurisdiction and I called to see if anything new has surfaced."

"Nothing solid."

Noah sensed the man holding something back and

he was determined to dig it out of him. "I'd appreciate anything you can give me, including your opinion."

"Fine, but be aware this is pure conjecture. I don't have a shred of evidence to back it up."

"Understood."

"It's just interesting that these incidents began after her husband was killed in a car crash several years ago. There were no other cars involved. It happened in the Blue Ridge Mountains and he went over a cliff for no apparent reason. The car was checked thoroughly and Mr. Mayfield was tested for drugs and alcohol. Everything came out clean as a whistle."

"What led you to check on the husband's death?"

"I interviewed everyone connected to Abigail Mayfield and came up empty, so I dug deeper. Turns out Mr. Mayfield had a big life insurance policy and that's why I checked on his death."

Goose bumps pricked Noah's arms. "How much?"

"I'll put it this way. Ms. Mayfield is a wealthy woman by most people's standards. Her husband was insured for half a million tax-free dollars. There was nothing to indicate foul play regarding her husband's death, and I couldn't find one person who had anything bad to say about Ms. Mayfield. The whole thing doesn't make any sense."

"I appreciate the information."

"Let me know what you find out and call if I can help in any way."

Noah slowly tucked his cell phone back in his pocket.

Was Abigail Mayfield the innocent choir director and piano teacher she appeared to be, or did she have a sinister side? One capable of murdering her husband for monetary gain?

With these unsettling thoughts in mind, Noah

watched Ms. Mayfield descend the stairs. He followed
her out the front door and waited while she locked the
house behind them. They climbed into his patrol car
and he headed toward Blessing's one and only church.
His mind ran a gauntlet of different scenarios. He'd
witnessed the underbelly of society during his tenure
at the FBI, and nothing would surprise him, but deep
down he didn't believe—or want to believe—that Abby
was capable of such violence. Her voice brought him
out of his musings.

"Okay, I'm a straightforward woman, Sheriff Galloway, and I want you to lay your cards on the table so
we can get past whatever's bothering you."

She surprised him with her frankness. "How did you
know something was bothering me?"

"Sheriff—"

"Call me Noah."

"Fine. Noah, and if we're going to be spending time
together, you can call me Abby. Now, spill."

He grinned. He couldn't help it. Abby might look
like a beautiful rose, but the woman had grit and he did
want answers. "I just spoke to Sheriff Brady."

Eagerness filled her voice. "Has he found any more
information on the occurrences in North Carolina?"

"Not exactly."

"What, exactly, did he say?" Exasperation replaced
her enthusiasm.

"He hasn't found any new information on your case,
but he did bring your husband's death into question."

"What?" Genuine bewilderment came off her in
waves.

Noah didn't think she could fake that. "During the
investigation, Sheriff Brady didn't come across one person in your life who came under suspicion. Because of

that, he expanded his investigation and discovered your husband had a rather large insurance policy."

Silence filled the car. Noah took his eyes off the road for an instant and glanced at Abby. Her face had turned an alarming shade of red and she looked ready to explode. Easing the car to the side of the road, he brought the vehicle to a stop.

"Are you alright?"

"Am I alright? No, I'm not alright. Are you telling me Sheriff Brady thinks I would murder my husband for such a piddly amount of money? I'll tell you this right now, my husband was a good man, and he was worth a whole lot more than half a million dollars."

Big fat tears rolled down her cheeks and Noah felt like a heel. Abby was either playing on his sympathy or she was telling the truth. He wanted to believe the latter. Her emotions were too raw.

"And I'll tell you another thing that only my grandmother knows. I was pregnant when my husband died." She pulled a Kleenex out of her purse and blew her nose. Her voice wobbled when she spoke again. "I lost the baby not long after he died. I was devastated. I-it was a baby boy. And just so you know, I used part of the money to move to Texas, put some aside to take care of my grandmother as she grows older and gave a substantial amount to a local orphanage in memory of my son."

Noah felt bad for even bringing it up. "Ms. Mayfield—Abby—I believe you. I'm sorry I brought up such painful memories."

She blew her nose again. "Thank you."

"Truce?"

She gave him a tremulous smile. "Truce. Now, get me to choir practice before I'm late." Her tone was filled with false bravado, but he let it go.

He guided the car back onto the road. "Yes, ma'am."

The church was only five minutes away and Noah canvassed the outer perimeter of the church grounds as Abby hurried up the front steps of the building. A few minutes later he slipped inside, slid into a pew at the back of the church and settled in. He counted twenty people and wondered if Joanne Ferguson and Walter Fleming were in attendance. He really didn't think they were involved, but he'd ask Abby to introduce them before everyone left.

His attention was drawn to Abby's elegant hands as they flowed over the keys of the antique baby grand piano. He wondered how a church this small had raised enough money for such a nice piano, and then it hit him. Abby's piano at home was a Steinway and he suspected she had purchased the church's piano with part of the insurance money. He would check out the orphanage donation, but he believed her. His internal antenna had convinced him she was innocent.

He subtly checked out each choir member. They were all smiling and seemed to appreciate the work Abby was doing as their director. His attention zoomed in on a guy seated in the back row. He had a strong, male voice that rose above the others.

The man had to be Walter Fleming. He was tall and distinguished looking. The guy would be right at home working as a banker.

Noah closed his eyes as the old hymns he remembered from childhood washed over him. A peace he hadn't felt in a long time settled in his soul and he breathed deeply.

He really wished—

The music stopped and he opened his eyes as Abby said a closing prayer before the group started to disperse. Several people spoke to him as they left, and he stood when Abby scurried down the aisle—the woman did everything so energetically—with the tall, distinguished man at her side.

"Noah—Sheriff Galloway—I don't believe you've met Walter Fleming." Her words came out in a rush. Subterfuge was not one of Ms. Mayfield's—Abby's—finer points.

"Walter, the sheriff gave me a ride to church, and since you're new in town, I thought you'd like to meet him."

The man had a firm handshake. "Nice to meet you, Walter."

Walter nodded briskly. "You, too, Sheriff." Fleming patted Abby on the shoulder and Noah stiffened as a jolt of jealousy shot through him. It was unwarranted. He'd only known the woman for two days. He contributed the feeling to being her protector. "I'll see you early Sunday morning if you don't mind running my part for me again before the service."

"I'll be happy to. See you then."

Fleming left and Noah raised a brow at Abby.

She huffed out a breath. "I thought you'd want to meet him."

Noah grinned. "I did. Good work. I take it Joanne Ferguson wasn't here?"

"No. And she didn't call or email, either. I hope nothing's wrong."

"Well, let's get you home."

As they were leaving, something struck the old wooden door behind them, mere inches from Abby's head.

Noah knew exactly what the sound meant. He

grabbed Abby, twisted her around, threw open the church doors and shoved her back inside the building.

A multitude of emotions crashed through him as he held Abby, wrapped in the safety of his arms, against the back of the closed door. He had a burning desire to protect her. Fear for her well-being roiled through him. She trembled and his emotions intensified.

"It's okay."

She pulled out of his arms, took a deep breath and lifted her chin. He admired a woman who could pull herself together so soon after being shot at.

"Did someone just—"

"Yes. Someone shot at you and they used a silencer. It suggests a professional hit."

Her eyes rounded, but it didn't take long for her to take in the information. Tight fists landed on her hips and her eyes narrowed. "I want to catch the person doing this." Noah moved back when she took a step forward. "I'm tired of being afraid to look over my shoulder. I can use myself as bait and lure whoever is after me out into the open. It's time to set up a sting operation."

It took a moment for her words to penetrate his brain. "Absolutely not. It's too dangerous. There's a good chance we're dealing with a professional killer."

Her shoulders slumped, her face crumbled and his heart melted. Those adorable, soft brown eyes found his. "What am I supposed to do? I can't live like this the rest of my life."

"Let's deal with tonight first. I'll call Cooper. He'll check the grounds of the church and we'll get you home." Her eyes shimmered with unshed tears and it was his undoing. "Trust me to help you, Abby. This is what I do." The corner of his mouth lifted. "I'm very good at my job."

She nodded and he reached for his cell phone. Before he had a chance to call his deputy, he heard the familiar sound of a timer going off. He grabbed Abby, shoved her back out the church doors and down the front steps, and shielded her body with his as they hit the ground.

The explosion in the church covered Abby's scream. The shooter wasn't trying to kill her with a bullet, he'd wanted them back inside the church where all evidence would be destroyed in the fire. A second, fiercer explosion lit the night sky. Someone wanted Abby Mayfield dead and they were willing to blow up a church to make it happen.

FIVE

Abby spit dirt out of her mouth and coughed as she tried to lift her head. Her eyes felt scorched and her throat burned from the smoke. She could barely breathe beneath the heavy weight covering her.

Noah! Is he okay?

Facedown on the ground, she tried to move, but froze when he stirred on top of her. Relief slammed through her when he whispered against her neck, "Don't move. If the shooter is still here, we want him or her to think we're dead."

Her heart slammed against her chest and she whispered a quick prayer. She wasn't ready to die, and Noah had a son to raise. It would be her fault if that sweet young boy was orphaned. "Dear Lord, please, please, please keep us safe until help arrives."

Noah stayed quiet and Abby took short, gasping breaths until a siren wailed in the distance. Within minutes, Cooper's patrol car swerved into the church parking lot and skidded to a stop. Noah's deputy opened the driver's door and took position, using the door as cover, his gun raised through the open window. Abby's fear and tension lessened when soft lips moved against her neck.

"At least Cooper followed proper procedure. There might be hope for my deputy, after all."

Her anxiety lessened, but there was someone who wanted her dead badly enough to blow up a church, and they might still be out there. A shiver of fear racked her body and she hated it. She'd never been afraid of anything and she refused to start now. She had faith that God was in control and Noah would solve the mystery surrounding her. He didn't know it yet, but she was going to help him. Her grandmother had always taught her to face fear head-on.

A passing thought of the beautiful, Steinway baby grand piano that she had donated to the church—now burning to ashes along with the rest of the building— brought forth a blaze of fury.

"Abby, can you get up and run to the car?"

"You bet I can." She swiped the hair out of her eyes. "I'm fine, just shaken."

"Here's what we're going to do. On the count of three, I want you to stand as fast as you can and run to the car. Jump in through the driver's-side door, climb into the back seat and lay down on the floor. I'll be right behind you."

He didn't give her time to think. He counted to three and she scrambled to her feet. He used his body as a protective shield as she stumbled to the car. Once inside, she crawled into the back seat and nose-dived to the floor.

She heard Noah whispering instructions to his deputy.

"Looks like the shooter is gone, but we won't take any chances. You cover me to the tree line. I'm going to check the perimeter of the property. I know the general trajectory of the bullet. The perp was up high, possibly perched in a tree."

Abby squeezed her eyes shut when Cooper gave a shaky response. "Are you sure, Sheriff? I've got a bad feeling about this."

"Cooper, you've been trained for this and you can do it. Stay focused and cover me."

Noah's voice oozed authority, command and encouragement. A true leader. In that moment, Abby's heart—one that had slammed shut after losing her husband and unborn child—opened just the tiniest bit.

She prayed until she heard Noah's voice.

"All clear."

She didn't know how much time had passed, but finally another siren wailed in the distance and Noah spoke again. "I don't think there's going to be much left for the fire truck to save."

Abby closed her eyes against an invasion of disbelief and devastation. *Fire truck*, as in *one*? Blessing's only house of worship was burning to the ground and it was her fault. The building, over a hundred years old, had tremendous historical value. It was irreplaceable.

The back door of the patrol car opened and Noah held out a hand. She grabbed it and allowed him to help her from the floor and out of the vehicle. Both of them coughed and stood in morbid silence, watching as four firemen fought to douse the flames.

God's house was slowly being reduced to a smoldering heap of burning timber. Abby curled her hands at her sides and gritted her teeth. "This is my fault. I led whoever is after me to Blessing and now they've destroyed the church."

Before Noah could offer platitudes, she turned to

him. Soot covered his face, but she didn't see any burns. "You saved my life. Are you okay?"

"Abby, this isn't your fault. We'll find the person responsible."

"Yes, we will, and they're going to go to jail for burning this beautiful building. And my piano."

Cooper joined them. "The fire chief says it's a total loss. I hope the church has insurance." A sad, quiet moment passed as they stood, staring at the burning building.

Abby spoke up first. "I'm now taking an active role in this investigation, so get used to it."

His sudden grin threw her off balance.

"What?"

His smile widened. "Ever since meeting you, I've thought of you as a steel magnolia. A sweet Southern belle with a spine of steel."

The description stunned her for a moment, but then she realized she liked it. She liked it a lot. "You can thank my grandmother for the steel side of my personality. At least you didn't call me Tinker Bell."

"Now that you mention it—"

"Don't even say it."

The next morning, Abby cracked her eyes open and carefully stretched her body to work out the kinks. Before going to bed, she had taken a long, hot shower to get rid of the horrid, smoky stench and relax her muscles. Hitting the hard ground and having a large man slam his body on top of hers had left a few bruises. But she wasn't complaining. Noah had saved her life.

Bates jumped on the bed, sat on his haunches and stared at her. She chuckled at the dog's antics. "Come on, Bates, baby, give Mama a morning snuggle. I sure could use one."

He licked her face and rooted his nose against her neck. She laughed, but after a few minutes pushed the dog away. "Enough. I have to get moving. I have a ton of things to do today."

The familiar interlude put things in perspective.

Abby put the finishing touches on her makeup and wondered if Noah was up. He had insisted on staying in her guest bedroom—she would *never* tell Grammy that a man she wasn't married to had stayed in her house overnight. The doorbell rang, and Bates was already standing at attention in front of the door when she hit the top of the stairs. The dog was alert but not concerned. He always stayed quiet, but she was beginning to understand his body language. The person ringing her doorbell was not an enemy.

Noah sped out of the kitchen just as she reached the foyer. "I asked Cooper to bring me some clothes."

She smiled. "Good morning, Sheriff."

He didn't smile back. Something was wrong. He opened the door and there stood Cooper with a suitcase in hand.

"Got here as soon as I could, Sheriff. Ms. Newsome's cat got stuck in a tree again and I had to get him down. Sam's an ornery old tabby. Bit me on the hand while I was rescuing him."

Noah grabbed the suitcase. "Thanks. Call if you need me."

He was about to shut the door but Abby scooted around him. She frowned at Noah as she passed and then blessed Cooper with a big smile. "Would you like to come in and have a cup of coffee?"

Cooper reacted to the dark look on Noah's face. "No,

ma'am. I appreciate it, but I have to get back to the station."

The deputy practically ran off the porch before Abby could say a word. She rounded on Noah. "That was rude."

He ignored her and turned toward the kitchen. "Come on. I got a pot of coffee going."

She followed him, fixed a cup for herself and sat down across from him. They stared at each other. The situation reminded her of two circling dogs. She didn't care for the suspicious look in his eyes. She'd always been a straightforward person, and she leaned on that trait now, even as her heart plummeted.

"Spit it out, Sheriff. I have a right to know what's going on."

Noah wanted to believe Abby Mayfield was exactly who she claimed to be, but during his tenure at the FBI, he'd learned things were seldom as they appeared. He had to separate his emotions from the facts and do his job.

Firming his resolve, he organized his thoughts and maintained a mask of professionalism. "I need more information on your parents' histories. Did they always live in North Carolina, or is it possible they lived elsewhere before you were born? Anything you can remember will help."

Her lips formed a tight line and her eyes narrowed. Noah leaned back in his chair, waiting for the steel part of the steel magnolia to come alive.

"You don't believe me, do you?" Her voice lowered. "I told you the truth. My parents were both only children. They grew up in North Carolina and lived near the Winston-Salem area their entire lives. I grew up in the small town of Mocksville. Grammy is my only living relative and that's it. I'll swear on a stack of Bibles if that's what it takes to convince you."

Anger left her chest heaving, searching for air. Was she telling the truth? He couldn't afford to take her at face value.

"That won't be necessary."

Her hands curled into fists on top of the table and she glared at him. "And to think I was starting to like you."

Noah had never second-guessed himself in the past, and he couldn't understand why he was doing it now. Was he making a mistake by not believing her? Before he had a chance to respond, she stretched out her fingers, relaxed her hands and wiped all emotion from her face, mimicking his behavior. The loss of her smile, even her anger, left him feeling disgruntled.

"I'm sorry, that was inappropriate. I don't know what I was thinking. I assume you came across new information that accounts for your reaction. Please share what you found and I'll do my best to answer any questions you may have."

His throat tightened. He didn't want to upset her, but the information he'd found earlier while doing a search on her parents didn't look good.

"I ran your parents' names through our database." He hesitated. If she was innocent, this new information would bring chaos to her life.

"Yes?"

He cleared his throat. "Based on federal and state records, your parents' and grandmother's total history begins in 1987."

He watched her closely. Her eyes rounded and he could almost see her brain working through those soft brown eyes, connecting the dots.

"That's the year I was born."

He nodded in agreement. "Before 1987, there's no record of either of your parents or your grandmother. They were easy to find because they were the only Mayfields living in Mocksville, but I'm going to need any information you can lay your hands on."

Her face crumbled. His gut clenched when her eyes filled with moisture, but it didn't surprise him when she straightened her shoulders and blinked away the unshed tears. In a short amount of time, he already knew her well enough to anticipate her responses.

"I'll get you the information you need, Sheriff, but I'm certain there's been a mistake, and I'll prove it."

SIX

Abby was afraid her heart would pound right out of her chest. There had to be a mistake. Faint memories of her parents swirled in her head. Their home had been filled with laughter, and for the short amount of time she had with them, she'd always been at the center of their circle of love. Her dad had claimed Abby was a duplicate of her mother and declared how blessed he was to have two such beautiful women in his life. She recalled a lot of laughter and a ton of love even though she'd been only six years old when they died.

Shadows moved through her mind. There were also a few times she'd overheard her parents in private conversation, her mother crying in her father's arms.

She shoved the memories aside. Noah had to be mistaken. Abby had a sudden, desperate urge to see Grammy. She needed the comfort her grandmother would offer. Someone who believed in her and would stand by her side through this mess.

She'd have to cancel her students' piano lessons for that day. Her thoughts racing, she looked at Noah. He didn't trust her, and right now she wanted to get rid of him so she could think things through.

"If that's all, I have a full day ahead of me. I'll notify

you as soon as I gather the information I have on my parents." She heard the frost in her tone, but couldn't help it. She had the sickening feeling Sheriff Galloway's investigation was getting ready to blow her life apart.

He shook his head. "I'm not leaving your side until we find out what's going on."

Abby took a deep breath and steeled her resolve. "I appreciate everything you've done, but I have Bates and I'm proficient with a gun. I want you to leave. If you refuse, I'll call your boss, who I assume to be the mayor, and tell him to ask you to leave."

Her heart was pounding. She really needed time to process the information he'd unearthed and she wanted to speak to her grandmother in private. Grammy was the only one left who could answer questions about her family history and why there was no information about them before 1987.

With a locked jaw, he stood. "Fine."

That's all he said. He gathered his jacket and suit-case on the way out. Abby unplugged the coffeemaker and made several phone calls to her students. Quickly packing a bag, she called Bates to her side and locked the front door behind her. She'd been fortunate to catch a flight to Charlotte at the last minute. It was expensive, but she was anxious to get to Mocksville. She had a burning desire to talk to Grammy. Abby had the sinking feeling her grandmother knew more about her parents than she let on.

She opened the driver's door and threw a carry-on bag onto the back seat, ready to cue Bates to load his lovely self into the car, but spotted something on the seat. The dog released a low growl when Abby tensed, staring at the item in horror. It couldn't be.

She slowly backed away. Her life was spinning out of control and nobody seemed able stop the madness.

Noah sat in his patrol car on the opposite side of the street in front of Abby's house. He refused to leave her vulnerable to whoever was creating havoc in her life. He visualized his wife as Sonya lay dying in a cold, sterile hospital room. He wouldn't allow someone else to die on his watch.

Lost in thought, he almost missed Abby as she opened the front door, pulling a small suitcase. The dog trotted along beside her. Anger ripped through him. She was leaving town, which reinforced his suspicions. Distressed at being proven right, Noah flung the car door open, ready to confront her. Then he saw her slowly back away from the car.

Fear and adrenaline propelled him forward. He instinctively had his weapon in hand, positioned at his side, ready for action. He checked the area around them before approaching. Her eyes were focused intently on the car and she didn't acknowledge him. Bates lifted his head, but allowed Noah to move close.

He touched her arm, trying not to startle her. "Abby, it's Noah. Everything's okay. I need you to tell me what's going on."

Her chin lifted and Noah almost lost it when he caught sight of a tear rolling down her cheek.

"Noah?"

"Yes, it's me. I hadn't left yet and I saw you backing away from your car."

She took a deep breath, steadied her voice and pointed at the car. "I don't understand any of this."

"Tell me what happened."

"Someone left another picture. It's on my car seat.

It caught me off guard, but I didn't want to touch anything."

Noah moved close to the car and pulled out a handkerchief. Lifting the photo by a corner, he held it up. This one wasn't framed, and it was a different picture of Abby's parents and the child. The small family stood in the middle of a field—nothing in the background that could reveal their location. Noah got a sick feeling in his stomach. He suspected the couple had only taken pictures that couldn't be traced to a specific location.

"We'll check for prints, but I don't expect to find anything."

Abby nodded. He felt callous, interrogating her after she'd been through more trauma, but he needed answers. "Are you going somewhere, Abby?" He gentled his tone, but her eyes flashed and relief punched him in the chest. Her spunky self was sputtering to life.

"It's really none of your business, since I'm completely innocent in all this," she said. Then added in a dark undertone, "I'll be happy to tell you I'm going for a visit with Grammy."

And why is she hurrying off to North Carolina right after I questioned her about her parents? "I'm coming with you." He wanted answers and Abby was in danger, whether she knew more than she was telling or not. He'd also get a chance to question the grandmother about Abby's parents.

Maybe Abby's truly innocent in all of this and her grandmother holds the answers.

"What? You can't come with me."

He crossed his arms over his chest. "I'm knee-deep in this investigation. You want answers? I'm going to find them."

"What about Blessing? You're the only sheriff. And your son, you can't just leave him."

"Cooper can take care of Blessing, and Grandpa Houston will babysit Dylan."

She threw her hands in the air. "Fine, but Bates and I are getting on that airplane whether you're there or not."

"Abby, listen to me. Someone has made several attempts on your life. You're in danger, and my gut is telling me the pictures and the threats against your life are two separate occurrences."

She stilled. "What do you mean?"

It disturbed him to frighten her, but she had to know the truth. "Think about it. Whoever wants you dead has been forthright in their attempts. Why would they taunt you with pictures of your parents holding an unknown child in their arms? It feels like two separate issues."

"I don't know why any of this is happening." She lifted her chin. "The whole thing is crazy. I don't have an enemy in the world."

"Let me help you, Abby. We'll find the answers."

She nodded and his stomach settled. He didn't want to examine his motives too closely. He had a burning desire to protect her and he wanted answers. That's all he'd allowed himself to think of at the moment.

"Okay." Her quiet answer tugged at his heart, but he ignored it. "I'll call the airline, change my flight and get you a ticket."

After changing her flight and getting a ticket for Noah, Abby closed her bedroom door behind her and rubbed her temples. She'd fled to her room on the pretext that she'd forgotten to pack something. She just needed a few minutes to herself. It'd be a wonder if she didn't end up with a headache. Bates whined, garnering her attention. His eyes, a startling amber, were focused intently on her.

Her life had been flipped upside down and she didn't know which way to turn. Kneeling, she wrapped her arms around her precious baby boy. The Malinois breed was known for its intelligence and fierce protection abilities, but Abby had discovered a soft side to hers. Bates wanted to be with his people and was the most loving dog she'd ever been around. She needed that affection now, more than ever.

She laughed when he nuzzled her throat. She often wondered if he wanted to feel her heartbeat. Sometimes she woke up at night with his neck draped across hers.

"Oh, Bates, baby, my life is in chaos." With his soft, warm body leaning against her chest, she closed her eyes. "Dear Jesus, please show me the truth and protect me. I don't have any idea what's going on, but I know You surely do."

All the horrible, recent events clouded her mind. She analyzed what Noah had said about there being two separate factors involved. The more she thought about it, the more she became convinced he was right.

She had prayed for God to show her the truth, but did she really want to know? She shook off that negative thought. Of course she did.

Bates followed her downstairs where Noah was waiting by the front door. She tried to hang on to the angst she'd been harboring, but it fled at the sight of him. "I apologize for getting angry earlier. I'm not upset with you. I know it's your job to follow up on all leads and unexplained circumstances. We'll talk to Grammy. She can answer any questions you might have."

His gaze softened and he touched the brim of an imaginary hat. "I appreciate that, ma'am."

Her smile widened. "Why don't you wear a cowboy hat? Everyone else around here does."

"No particular reason. We better get going."

"Right."

Noah grabbed the handle of her small carry-on suitcase and Abby called her companion, "Bates, come on, baby. It's time to go see Grammy."

The once-proud dog slunk into the foyer with his tail tucked between his legs.

Noah's brows raised. "What's wrong with him? And is that a—"

"Bates is afraid to fly, so we got him certified as a service dog so he can stay in the passenger section of the plane with me. He can also go anywhere he pleases as long as he wears his cute little vest."

Noah appeared flummoxed and Abby sighed. She got that reaction from a lot of people.

After loading up in the car, and a quiet hour on the road, they were finally seated in the bulkhead of the plane with Bates shivering at her feet.

"I have to say I'm impressed with your airport savvy."

She grinned. "After my first trip with Bates, I learned to get my confirmation number first, then tell them about the dog. So far, they've always moved us to the exit seats where there's more legroom."

After takeoff, Bates settled down and Abby leaned her head back. "So, tell me, Noah, why do you think there's two different people involved in what's been happening? I agree with you, but I'm interested in hearing your thoughts on the subject."

Sitting in a row to themselves, their small section of the plane felt secluded and cozy to Abby. Like their own private world. A time and place where secrets could be shared. But until her parents' names were cleared, she didn't feel like sharing. She wasn't angry, but matters still didn't sit well between them.

"Think about it. You've had three break-ins, and someone tried to run you down with a car. You were shot at and the church exploded. We barely got out alive. Why would the person, or persons, behind that leave you pictures of your parents with an unknown child? Their intent was indicative of murder. These people aren't playing games. In my opinion, the pictures were left by someone else."

A cold chill iced her body. "But why would someone leave those pictures? It's just cruel."

The tension gathering in her body was producing a headache.

"It's okay, Abby. I promise we'll find out who's trying to harm you and who's leaving the pictures. I won't rest until we dig out the truth."

A chill snaked up her spine. That's what she was afraid of. The truth didn't always set a girl free.

SEVEN

Noah gripped the steering wheel of the rental car with one hand and grabbed his phone off the console when it rang. He cringed when he checked the caller ID. Just the person he didn't want to talk to. Now or ever.

Abby sent him a questioning look as he answered the call. He knew from past, painful experiences, if he didn't pick up, his father would keep pestering him.

"Hello, Dad."

Abby became absorbed in the passing scenery, but he knew she was listening.

"No, I'm not at the office. I'm out of town working on a case…That's none of your business…No, Grandpa Houston is taking care of Dylan."

His father's surly tone and blistering words filled his ear. Years of pent-up anger flooded him, same as it always did when his father called. He didn't need this right now, and he sure didn't want Abby to know about his dysfunctional family.

He lowered his voice. "I don't care how long you've been sober, you're not seeing my son. I have to go." Noah hung up on his father and gently set the phone back down, even though he wanted to put a fist through the windshield.

"You love Dylan very much."

"Yes, I do."

"You want to talk about it?"

"No. Yes. I—"

They had a tail. Noah checked the car's rearview mirror several more times and Abby caught on quick.

"Noah, what is it? What's wrong?"

"Someone is following us in a beige sedan. I spotted it at the airport, but didn't become suspicious until it followed us off the interstate."

She took a deep, steadying breath. Noah disliked scaring her, but she needed to be ready if he had to floor it.

"Maybe they're also headed to Mocksville."

"Let's just say I have a reliable instinct when it comes to these kinds of things, and it's screaming right now. Hold on."

Abby gasped and grabbed her door handle when he took a sharp right onto a side road. Three cars behind them, the sedan must have realized he'd been seen and gave up all pretense of the charade. The larger car sped up and rammed their bumper. Abby stayed quiet, but Bates growled from the back seat.

"Hold on." Wishing he had his patrol car with the big, high-powered V-8 engine, Noah stepped on the gas, but the sedan was faster and quickly closed the gap. At least they were on a country road where traffic was scarce.

"Noah, there's a sharp curve ahead with a steep drop-off on the right side. There's been a lot of wrecks there." Noah appreciated the fact that Abby had a level head and wasn't falling apart. Within moments the curve was in sight.

There was nowhere to go, with a steep embankment on the left and a deep gully on the right. The sedan took his choices away when it sped up and came alongside their car. Noah cut the steering wheel and rammed the vehicle, but the small compact did little damage.

He knew what was coming next. "Abby, hold tight. We're going over the embankment." A second later the sedan slammed into his side of the car and then sped ahead.

He caught part of the plate number right before their vehicle sailed through the air. There was a beat of absolute silence, suspended in time, until the moment of impact.

An airbag exploded in his face along with the sound of metal slamming against hard ground. His seatbelt strained against his chest and he knew the car had balanced on the front end. Half a second later, the back end slammed back to earth, making his teeth rattle.

"Abby! Are you okay?"

She didn't answer and Noah waged a war against his airbag. Barely able to reach his jeans pocket, he struggled to gain hold of his pocketknife. Jabbing a hole in the airbag, he frantically swatted it out of the way. His heart almost stopped when he saw Abby. Her airbag had failed to deploy and she had a nasty gash on her temple. Her eyes were closed and blood ran down the side of her face.

"Abby!" He reached over to check her pulse and a low, menacing growl rose from the back seat. With slow, precise movements, he turned and faced the animal. The dog's lips were peeled back, revealing a mouthful of sharp, canine teeth. He'd never heard such a vicious snarl. The dog was in full protection mode. His heart raced. Abby wasn't conscious and he had to get her to the hospital. Head injuries could be serious.

"Bates, you know me, boy. I have to help Abby. Can you calm down?"

A long, low growl was his response. Bates stood on all fours in the back seat, fur bristling. The dog could rip Noah's throat out in a second flat.

He hadn't prayed in a long time, didn't even know if it would do any good, but it couldn't hurt. He closed his eyes. "God, if You're really up there, Abby needs Your help in a bad way." It wasn't much of a prayer, but then again, Noah didn't expect much of an answer. But maybe He would help Abby.

His eyes still closed, a memory of Abby calling her dog off the first time they met surfaced with gentle clarity. Would it work?

He opened his eyes and met Bates's stare. In a light tone, he murmured, "Bates, baby, you be nice now."

The dog quit growling, canted his head at Noah and then sat back on his haunches.

Noah didn't take the time to examine his prayer too closely, he was too concerned about Abby's condition. Keeping a close eye on the dog, he leaned across the console and laid two fingers against her throat. She was alive! Relief washed over him. It was more than relief, but he didn't take time to analyze those feelings.

Confident that Bates was under control, Noah searched the floorboards for his cell phone. He found it by running his hand under the seat. Fumbling, he almost dropped it when he dialed.

"Nine-one-one. What's your emergency?"

He breathed deeply to steady himself and brought his training into focus. Abby sitting beside him, unconscious, with blood running down her face, was almost his undoing.

"This is Sheriff Noah Galloway visiting from Blessing, Texas. There's been an accident and you need to send an ambulance right away. I don't know the name of the road we're on, so you'll have to track us via GPS on my cell phone."

"I'm setting up the tracking system right now. What's the nature of your injury?"

"I'm fine. Just bruised up. My passenger, Abby Mayfield, is the one who's hurt. Her airbag didn't release. She has a head injury."

"I'm sure you know not to move her."

"Yes, ma'am. There's something else you should know. We were forced off the road by another vehicle. I was able to get a partial plate number—*C* as in *cat*. *A* as in *apple*. And *M* as in *man*. C-A-M."

"We've tracked your position. The ambulance and patrol cars are on their way. Stay on the phone until they arrive."

"Yes, ma'am."

Noah jerked when Abby groaned. "N-Noah?"

Bates laid his head on the back of Abby's seat and whined.

Noah leaned across the console and placed his hand against her cheek. "You're okay. Just stay still until the ambulance arrives. Everything's okay."

"Bates? Is he okay?"

The dog raised up over the seat and licked her.

She chuckled and winced at the same time. "My head hurts." She raised a hand to her temple, but Noah gently stopped her.

"Your airbag didn't work and you banged your head. You're going to have a terrible headache before this is over, but we're okay."

She turned toward him and winced again. "And you? Are you okay?"

"I'm fine. Just a few bruises."

Sirens wailed in the distance and he forced a smile. "Here comes the cavalry."

She grimaced. "What about the car that forced us off the road?"

He wanted to track down and slay whoever had done this to them, but he tamped down his fury and gentled his voice. "You don't need to worry." He couldn't stop his voice from hardening. "I'll find them, and when I do—"

"We'll find them, Noah, but don't let them fill you with hate. God has a way of working these things out."

They'd get worked out alright, but now was not the time to discuss it. He heard the sirens of the ambulance and patrol cars as they stopped on the road at the top of the gully. "Will you be okay if I get out of the car?"

She rallied. "Of course I'll be okay. You know I'm a GRITS girl."

At his raised brows, she explained, "You know, GRITS. Girls raised in the South. I'll show you my T-shirt sometime."

He grinned. The woman had more spunk than most men he knew. "I'd like that."

"Well, then, go. Shoo."

By the time Noah forced his door open, the police and EMTs had made their way down the embankment. The car was swarming with people and one guy took Noah by the arm. He shook off the man's grip and raced around to Abby's side of the car to make sure she was okay. They had her on her feet by the time he got there. He rushed to her side and glared at the EMT standing next to her.

The guy shrugged his shoulders. "She said she was okay and insisted on getting out before we could check her properly." The man's eyes rounded and he took several steps back when Bates hopped out beside Abby. The dog obviously took his cues from Abby and didn't growl at the guy.

Staying well away from the dog, the EMT addressed Abby. "Ma'am, do you think you can make it up the embankment with help, or do you need a stretcher?"

Noah answered for her, "She'll go up on a stretcher."

She raised a brow but, thankfully, didn't argue.

Abby would have taken issue with Noah's domineering attitude, but her body felt like someone had used it as a punching bag. The EMT had shaken his head when Abby insisted on getting out of the car, but she would know if something was broken. Two of the guys laid out a stretcher and Noah helped her onto it. She smiled and then winced when they strapped her in.

"Are you okay?" Concern clouded Noah's face.

"Don't worry so much. I'll be fine."

A tall distinguished-looking man clad in khakis and a starched white shirt came around the back of the car and hovered over Abby with both hands shoved into his pockets.

"Evening, Ms. Mayfield. Looks like trouble's found you again."

She gave him a sharp look. "Looks like you've been barking up the wrong tree, Sheriff Brady. So you think I had something to do with my husband's death, do you? When I prove you wrong, I'm going to send an article to the *Mocksville Observer* and let the decent, upstanding folks of this county know what kind of a job you've been doing."

Noah stepped between Abby and the sheriff with an extended hand. "Sheriff Galloway. It's nice to meet you, but we should get Abby to the hospital. We can talk there."

"Of course." Brady raised a brow at Abby and that burned her gut. "I'll need to get your statements."

Bates released a low growl. The dog sensed her distress. She reached over and brushed his fur. "It's okay, baby. Everything's fine now."

The EMTs, who had waited for permission from Sheriff Brady, lifted the stretcher at his nod. Bates followed as they moved toward the embankment. Noah called his name, but the animal ignored the summons and stayed glued to her side. Her muscles ached and her head throbbed as the two guys carrying her up the hill muttered back and forth about a dog not being allowed inside the ambulance or hospital.

Noah jogged up beside the stretcher and addressed the EMTs. "The dog goes with her. He's special needs certified and I'll clear it with the hospital when I arrive."

The crash caught up with her and Abby felt tired all of a sudden. "Thanks, Noah."

Her eyelids drooped as they loaded her into the ambulance. Lying prone, she had a good view of the pine trees growing on the steep incline to the left. A flash of gold caught her eye and she squinted. A man moved from behind a tree and trekked farther into the dense forest. She only saw the back of him. He had blond hair and wore jeans and a dark blue jacket. She had to tell Noah—what if the man was the one who had run them off the road?—but when she tried to form the words, her mind clouded with drowsiness and she welcomed the escape.

EIGHT

A big uproar ensued at the hospital over the dog, but Sheriff Brady pulled some strings and Noah was grateful. They sat waiting in the emergency room while the doctor checked Abby. A nurse looked Noah over and gave him a clean bill of health. He'd have a few sore muscles and several large bruises, but that was the extent of his injuries. He paced the floor while Brady sat on a hard plastic chair, coffee cup in hand.

"So, that's the way the wind blows, is it?"

Noah stopped midpace and his mind played catch-up. He'd been imagining all the horrible things that could result from a head injury.

"What?"

Brady propped his elbows on his thighs, both hands wrapped around his coffee cup. "You're interested in Ms. Mayfield."

Noah stiffened and faced the sheriff. "That's none of your business."

Brady leaned back in his chair and stretched out his legs, crossing them at the ankles. "From all appearances, Abby Mayfield appears to be a pillar of the community, but someone wants her dead and there has to be a reason."

"You haven't found one yet."

Brady winced at the truth, stood, stretched, and held out a hand. "I apologize for intruding into your personal business."

Noah hesitated, then shook Brady's hand. "Apology accepted."

They both took a seat.

"I ran your name through our database after you called from Texas. I'm impressed with your credentials. That was quite a coup you had, saving the mayor's life in New York."

"Yes, well, there's always a price to be paid. It comes along with the notoriety."

"Yes, well, you have your hands full with Ms. Mayfield." Brady raised his hands in surrender when Noah's face clouded. "Just saying. I take it you haven't met her grandmother? The old lady's a spitfire if I ever saw one."

Before the conversation disintegrated, Abby was wheeled into the waiting room by a nurse, Bates trotting at her side. Noah rushed toward her. Her blond hair had been pulled back into a ponytail and she sported a large bandage on her left temple. "Are you okay? Do you hurt anywhere? What did the doctor say?"

Her lips curved and she tapped her forehead. "I'll live to see another day. No concussion, which is what the doctor was worried about. Just a few bumps and bruises. The painkiller they gave me is kicking in as we speak. God protected us."

Noah didn't know about God, but the tension that had been holding his body hostage eased off and he found he could breathe again.

Abby turned her attention to Sheriff Brady. "That wasn't very nice, what you just said about my grandmother."

Brady released a long sigh. "I apologize, ma'am."

Abby nodded, as if accepting his apology. "I have something to tell you. When they were loading me into the ambulance, I looked up the hill on the other side of the road and spotted a man in the woods."

Fear sliced a sharp edge through Noah's gut. Abby could have been taken out, right there on the side of the road. He should have been more diligent, but the car that ran them off the road had long disappeared. The driver hadn't had time to circle back, hide the car and trek through the woods. Who was the man in the trees, and how did he get there so fast? The driver had had no way of knowing Noah and Abby would turn on that country side road when they did. The only explanation? Someone besides the sedan had been following them. Abby's eyes widened in fear and he could see they had reached the same conclusion.

"There was someone else following us?" Her voice rose in volume and seeing Brady wince gave Noah a stingy amount of satisfaction.

"She sings a lot," Noah said.

"I can tell."

Abby wagged a finger at them. "I'm sitting right here."

And out comes the steel magnolia, Noah thought, and he was happy to see it make an appearance. He could deal with the feisty side of the woman much more easily than the vulnerable Tinker Bell. He reminded himself never to call her that out loud.

She lifted worry-filled eyes. "Did they—whoever is doing this—follow us from Texas?" She took a deep breath, as if girding herself for what she was about to say. "Or is it more like a group thing, with several people involved? Do you think it's the same people who blew up the church?"

Sheriff Brady stiffened and his own tone rose in volume. "A church was blown up?"

Abby smirked at Brady, and Noah wanted to hug her when she said, "If you'd quit spending all your time trying to prove I did something to my husband for the insurance money, you might learn something."

Time for a referee, Noah thought. "Abby, why don't we calm down and give the sheriff our statements? We can fill him in on everything that's happened."

Abby mumbled under her breath as Noah wheeled her closer to the hard plastic visitor chairs. "Fine, but I'll sic Bates on him if he doesn't behave."

Noah laughed and Brady threw her a sharp look right before his cell phone rang. "Oh, and by the way, my officers are keeping an eye out for a beige sedan with the partial plate number you gave us. Maybe we'll find something. Sorry, I have to take this. It's the station." He moved a few steps away.

Taking a seat, Noah reached over and laid his hand over Abby's. Her skin felt cold to the touch. "We'll find who's doing this. I promise. And Sheriff Brady only wants to help."

Her lips firmed. "I just don't get it. Who is doing this and why? Nothing makes sense anymore."

He removed his hand from hers just as Brady got off the phone and clipped it back to his belt. Over Abby's shoulder, Noah's eyes met Brady's and he knew the news wasn't good.

He gave Brady a questioning look. "What is it?"

Abby glanced over her shoulder at the sheriff. "Is something wrong?"

"Your statements will have to wait. There's been a

break-in at your grandmother's house. A neighbor called dispatch when she spotted your grandmother crawling out the front door and onto the front lawn. She's in an ambulance on her way here."

A gasp filled the room and Abby's voice reached a higher crescendo than ever before. "Grammy's hurt? They broke into her home?" She stopped long enough to fill her lungs. Her voice lowered and her words came out low. "Those people dared to lay hands on my grandmother? I need to draw them out into the open and put an end to this farce once and for all."

He wouldn't allow it! Noah's heart almost jumped out of his chest at the thought of Abby placing herself in harm's way until Sheriff Brady stepped forward.

"Ms. Mayfield, I'm the law in this town, and we will not be using a civilian as bait. If I get wind that you're planning on doing any such thing, I'll put you in jail and keep you there for the duration of this investigation."

Abby scrunched up her face. "I'm going to the ER desk to wait on the ambulance. Everything can be put on hold until I see that Grammy's okay. Did your dispatcher say anything about her condition?"

Brady shook his head and Abby scuttled out of the room.

"It's time you and I have a talk."

Noah bristled at Brady's tone, but he had a good view through the room's plate glass windows of Abby harassing the poor woman at the check-in desk. Bates stood by her side. She shouldn't be out of the wheelchair and moving around like that. It was a blessing she didn't have a concussion.

"Sheriff Galloway?"

Shaking off his worry, he sat down and faced Brady.

It didn't take long to bring him up to speed, and the sheriff wasn't happy with the situation.

"Since moving to Texas, Ms. Mayfield's house has been broken into, she's been shot at and a church was blown up?"

"Yep, that about sums it up." Noah ignored the man's sarcastic edge and pulled out his phone. He wasn't above asking for help. Between keeping Abby safe and dodging the attempts on her life, he hadn't had time to follow up on leads. He punched in a secure number and it was answered on the second ring.

"Ridenhour."

"Alex, it's me."

"Well, I'll be a son of a gun. If it isn't the hero of the hour and my old partner." Alex had always enjoyed mimicking Noah's Texas drawl. It used to get on his nerves, but he kind of missed it now.

"Yeah, it's me. Got something I want to run by you."

"What? No 'hello, how's the wife and kids'?"

Noah held on to his patience by a very thin thread. "Hello. How're the wife and kids doing? And you don't deserve the wonderful woman you scammed into walking down the aisle with you." That wasn't really true. Alex was one of the most honest men he knew, and Noah had trusted him with his life on many occasions.

"They're doing great. When are you coming back to the FBI? I figured by now you'd be bored to tears down in Tombouctou, working as sheriff of a small town." Alex's clipped New York accent had returned in full force.

"You know why I'm living in Blessing, and things are working out just fine. Dylan is safe from Anthony Vitale, and that's all that matters." Time to get down to business. "I have a problem and I need your help."

"I'm listening."

"I need information and I need it fast." Noah gave him a condensed version of everything that had happened. "The only new people in Abby's life are a couple of choir members—Joanne Ferguson and Walter Fleming—recently moved to Blessing. I did a surface search and everything appeared to come up clean, but I don't have any other suspects and I don't have the time, or the resources, to do a deep search on my own."

His old partner whistled. "Did I say you were bored in that two-horse town? After what happened with New York's mayor, leave it to you to step right into the middle of another big case."

"It's not a big case. It's one woman with no known enemies, but someone is trying to kill her."

"My gut says different. I'll have Simon see what he can find on the Ferguson woman and Walter Fleming."

"At this point, that's all I have to go on. I'm tracking down other leads, Abby's grandmother being one of them, but the older woman's house was broken into about the same time we were run off the road. There's more than one person involved in this situation and I need answers fast. The attempts on Abby's life are escalating."

"I'll call Simon now."

Simon was the FBI's best computer geek, and if there was anything to be found, the wonder boy would root it out.

"Thanks."

Noah ended the call and faced Brady. The sheriff wouldn't be happy he'd called his buddy in the FBI, but that was tough. He'd do whatever it took to keep Abby safe, whether he trusted her or not, and after meeting

Brady, he was more inclined to trust Abby. The sheriff
had hit a dead end on the investigation, anyway.

After Nurse Ratchet sternly told Abby to sit down
and wait, she crossed her arms and stood in front of
the ER doors, watching the ambulances come and go.
She rubbed her arms. The reality of the car crash had
settled in. She was more angry than afraid for herself,
but she wanted her grandmother protected until the terrible people who had tried to kill her and hurt Grammy
were caught and locked behind bars.

She tried to hold on to the anger because it was so
much easier to deal with than the paralyzing fear she
had for her grandmother. Bates whined at her side and
she reached down to pet her faithful companion. "It's
okay, boy. God is in control and Noah's doing everything he can to find out what's going on."

She tensed when another ambulance careened into
the ER parking lot, but controlled herself and waited
until they unloaded the patient and rolled the stretcher
into the building.

"Grammy!" she cried when the stretcher—guided by
the EMTs—raced through the automatic sliding doors.
Her grandmother's beautiful silver hair was caked with
dried blood and she looked as if she'd aged twenty years
since Abby last saw her. With the sheet covering her,
the older woman looked as thin as a rail. Tears sprang
forth as Abby raced alongside the stretcher even though
the nurses told her to get out of the way and let them do
their job. They wheeled her grandmother into a cubicle
and whipped the curtains closed.

A nurse grabbed Abby's arm. "Ma'am, you have to
leave. The doctor will be here soon."

Abby faced the nurse and drew a deep, calming

breath. "Please, let me stay with my grandmother until the doctor comes. She's the only family I have left."

The nurse's hard look softened and she gave Abby a curt nod. "Just a few minutes and stay clear of the nurses as they prep the patient for the doctor."

"I promise." The nurse left and Abby carefully worked her way around the busy nurses to the top of the stretcher where her grandmother's head lay. Abby reached out and lightly rubbed a finger across her forehead. Leaning down, she whispered, "Oh, Grammy. I never should have left you. We're moving you to Texas to live with me as soon as you're able." A choked sob escaped and her grandmother's eyelids fluttered.

"Abby? Is that you, sweetheart?" Her words sounded weak and it broke Abby's heart. This was her fault. Guilt consumed her, but she managed a watery smile when those precious brown eyes—so similar to hers—opened to half-mast.

"It's me, Grammy. You're at the hospital and the doctor will be here soon. Everything will be okay."

A spark of spirit lit the older woman's eyes and her voice gained a tiny bit of strength. "Of course it will, girl. God will see to everything." Her grandmother winced in pain and nausea churned in Abby's gut. It was killing her to see the usually strong, vibrant woman lying helpless in bed. This should never have happened. Grammy had always been a rock of strength, and to be brought so low for no good reason...

Churning anger mixed with fear and Abby leaned close. "We'll catch whoever did this to you. That I can promise."

Her grandmother's eyes drifted closed, as if in prayer, then blinked open again. "Come closer, Abby-girl."

Abby leaned down further.

"Don't poke into things. It's too dangerous. And don't trust anyone." Her grandmother's words drifted away and she closed her eyes just as the doctor flung a curtain open and gave Abby a nasty stare.

"Get her out. Now!"

A nurse took her by the arm and gently led her away.

Frozen, she stood there, staring at the closed curtain, her grandmother's words echoing through her mind. What did she mean? *Don't poke into things. It's too dangerous. And don't trust anyone.*

Abby started shaking, and on a subliminal level, she was aware of Bates whining at her side, but she couldn't move. Childhood memories that had seemed insignificant at the time flooded her mind. Times when she'd questioned Grammy about her parents and fraternal grandparents. Her grandmother would always laugh, tell some sweet little story about them and then change the subject. Now, as an adult, Abby recognized how evasive the answers had been.

She had the sinking feeling that Grammy knew a lot more than she ever admitted. And then there was her grandmother's odd reaction when she found out Noah—a well-known FBI agent recognized for digging until he found the truth—would be investigating Abby's problems.

Grammy had told her not to trust anyone. Did that include Noah?

NINE

Overwhelmed by everything that had happened in such a short period of time, all Abby wanted was to find a place to hide and think things through. Events were spinning out of control and she needed some time to mull over everything. Grammy's last words lay heavy on her heart and greatly troubled her. Without a doubt, her grandmother knew more than she was telling. Much more.

Closing her eyes, she breathed deeply and sent up a quick prayer for guidance, strength and protection. Her nerves calmed at once and she could think rationally. She had to stay by Grammy's side. Her grandmother was the most important person in the world to her. She had to be okay. Abby didn't know what she'd do without the woman who had taken her in and raised her after her parents died when she was so young.

Footsteps trod down the hall and Abby knew without turning that it was Noah. She could feel his presence. Her back to him, she opened her eyes and took another calming breath, but almost choked when she caught sight of a man standing at the end of the hall in front of the exit to the stairwell.

He stood still for a few seconds, staring straight at her.

There was an odd look on his face…almost apologetic, and she had the strangest sense of familiarity. As Noah's footsteps came closer behind her, the guy gave a curt nod and turned to flee through the exit door. Her breath caught in her throat when she noticed the stranger's collar-length blond hair. It was him! The man hiding in the woods at the crash site. Her heart pounded so hard in her chest she was afraid it would burst. Who was he? Why was he following her? And, most important of all, why had he allowed her to see his face?

Abby's head pounded from her injury and she swayed on her feet. Two strong arms caught her from behind.

"Abby! What is it? What's wrong?"

As she staggered under the heavy weight of the last few days, that strange sense of the familiarity that the stranger had created made her want to check Grammy's house for leads, but she wanted to do it alone. What if she discovered something she didn't want Noah to see? Something that shed an unfavorable light on her family's name?

She felt herself being lowered to the floor and a worried voice penetrated her haze.

"Abby! Are you okay? What happened?"

Noah! Reality came rushing back and she took a few seconds to pull her thoughts together. Should she tell him about the stranger? She was certain the man fit into this mess somehow—at least, her gut was telling her he did—but the man she saw… Something inside her locked down when Grammy's words of warning surfaced in her brain.

Noah's voice rose in volume as he called for help. He looked down and she felt silly lying prone on the floor.

"I'm fine." She held out a hand. "Help me up."

He gave her an accusing frown. "You almost fainted and then you smiled. What's that about?"

He helped her to her feet but kept a reassuring arm around her waist.

"I couldn't help thinking," she improvised, "when you called the nurse, well, you have a beautiful baritone voice. You should sing in the choir."

He grimaced and she followed suit.

"Well, maybe after we rebuild the church you can join the choir," she added.

He faced her and placed both hands on her shoulders, his probing eyes staring deeply into hers. She could see why he was so good at his job. "Abby, something frightened you. What was it?"

Her heart told her to trust Noah, but she needed time to sort things out. He tucked a strand of hair behind her left ear. He would handle this whole mess if she gave him free reign, but Grammy had taught her to be a strong, self-reliant woman, so she pulled away.

She missed his warmth and the security of his embrace—even if it was just to help her to her feet—but she needed to stand strong. She wasn't stupid, though, and she was an honest, upright person. She'd never lie to him. "Yes, something did frighten me, but I'm okay now, and I need some time to think things through."

His eyes changed. There was a flash of something that closely resembled wariness, but his expression quickly became shuttered. His arctic-blue eyes turned to ice, making Abby wonder if she'd just made a big mistake by withholding information.

"You don't trust me." His voice was tightly controlled, revealing nothing.

She tried to make him understand. "I barely know you. It's not that I don't trust you. I just need to make sure Grammy's okay and think about everything that's happened."

With her eyes, she pleaded for him to understand. He responded by taking her arm and leading her back to the waiting room.

"Come on, we'll sort this out later. Sit down and I'll check the nurse's station, see if there's any word on your grandmother."

On the threshold of the room, Abby effectively stopped him by laying a hand on his arm. "Speaking of trust, Noah, I have to know. Do you believe I had anything to do with my husband's death?"

A moment's hesitation gave Abby her answer and she removed her hand. "You expect me to trust you, but you don't trust me."

He started to say something but clamped his mouth shut. "I'll check on your grandmother."

With a heavy heart, Abby ignored Sheriff Brady, who sent her a suspicious look, and sat in one of the hard plastic seats. She closed her eyes, laid a hand on Bates and prayed for Grammy.

On the way to the nurse's station, Noah took several deep, calming breaths. Something had upset Abby enough to make her come close to fainting, and the woman he knew had a backbone of steel. Definitely not fainting material. His fury simmered as he reached the front desk, but he forced a smile after the woman recoiled and rolled her chair away.

"Sorry I startled you. It's been a long day."

She returned his smile and rolled her chair back toward the desk. "You got that right. It's always crazy in the ER. Can I help you?"

He propped an elbow on the countertop, mimicking a relaxed state while, inside, his gut churned. "I'd like to check on the elderly lady, Althea Beauchamp, brought in recently. I'm here with her granddaughter."

She pecked on her computer. "Oh, yes. The doctor is with her, but he should be out soon. I'll let you know if I hear anything."

"Thanks."

Noah forced his body to relax and entered the waiting room. His anger quickly turned to amusement. Abby and Sheriff Brady sat there, glaring at each other. The steel magnolia was alive and well. The comical sight relieved the tension in his shoulders.

Like a punch to the gut, he realized he wasn't upset at Abby for not sharing information. His irritation stemmed from something much deeper, feelings he wasn't ready to examine too closely. His true anger was caused by the people threatening Abby.

Before Brady and Abby could kill each other with nasty looks, a harried doctor swept into the room. Dressed in green scrubs, he held a chart in one hand and focused on Abby. "Abigail Mayfield?"

Abby scrambled to her feet and Noah moved to her side as she faced the doctor.

"Is my grandmother okay?" Her words came out fast. Fury suffused him and his fists clenched at his sides once again. He wanted to fix this for her, but felt helpless to do so. He hoped with all his heart her grandmother would make it.

Noah was impressed when the doctor slowed his frantic pace and took his time answering.

"Your grandmother is a tough lady, but she's not out of the woods."

Abby opened her mouth, but the doctor held up a hand to stop her from speaking.

"She has multiple bruises and contusions on her body, but my main point of concern is the trauma to her brain. She has a buildup of fluid and I've placed her in an induced coma until we can resolve the problem."

Abby gasped. Noah looked at the doctor. "Anything else we should know?"

The doctor shook his head and Noah thanked him. He left the room as quickly as he'd entered. How did physicians handle this kind of emotional stress every day? He couldn't have done it but admired those who did.

"It's okay, Abby. Everything's going to be okay." He gave her a comforting hug, and her hair felt soft and silky in his hands.

Without warning, she jerked away and wiped her eyes with one angry swipe. "Everything's not okay! Grammy's in the hospital fighting for her life and some fanatical people I don't even know want me dead. The whole world has gone crazy. I'm a choir director and piano teacher—" her fist tapped her thigh in anger "—and I've never hurt anyone. Why is this happening to me?"

Her pain and frustration mimicked his own.

Color suffused her face and those soft brown eyes he'd come to adore turned flinty. "I'll say one thing, if we don't find some answers soon, I'm going to figure out a way to lure whoever is after me out into the open."

His mind immediately rejected the idea of Abby taking any kind of a risk and he hardened his own expression. "Over my dead body."

She gave him a dubious smile and patted his hand. He didn't trust the change in her demeanor for a second.

"I'm sure we'll find answers soon. Now, why don't you just run along and find a hotel room? I'm staying at Grammy's house and I'm sure you could use a good, hot meal."

The small spark in her eyes belied her sugary sweetness. She was trying to get rid of him. But why? Something had happened right before she almost fainted and he wouldn't rest until he found out what she was hiding.

"I don't think so. You're staying glued to my side until this thing is figured out. And you can't stay in a house that has just been broken into. It's a crime scene. We'll both stay at a hotel where it's safe."

She turned and included Brady in their conversation. "Sheriff Brady, I don't believe Sheriff Galloway has jurisdiction in your county, does he?"

Brady shook his head and stood. "He's right. You can't stay at your grandmother's and y'all beat anything I've ever seen." He held out his hand toward Noah. "I have everything I need for the time being on the hit-and-run. I'll keep you informed of any progress on the investigation. Let me know if you need any help on your end." He cast an annoyed glance at Abby. "You'll need it with this one and her grandmother."

Abby gasped and Noah shook the man's hand. Brady left the room.

"I can't believe he just left like that. I never have liked that man."

"He's just doing his job."

She sniffed. "Not very well, if you want my opinion." She changed the subject. "I'm going to check on Grammy and then we'll find a place to stay."

Abby wanted to weep as she stood by her grandmother's bed. The air was cool and the room was deathly quiet except for the beeps coming from several monitors at the head of the bed. Tubes crisscrossed in every direction.

God, please be with Grammy. Let her live. She's all I have left.

Noah moved to Abby's side. "From what you've told me, your grandmother's a fighter. She'll make it."

"You don't know that."

"If she's anything like her granddaughter, she's strong enough to handle a bump in the road and come out fighting."

Standing beside her, he gave her a sense of rightness. Even though he didn't trust her—and she didn't care to have a relationship with someone in a life-threatening profession—for some strange reason it felt right. Maybe she should tell him about the blond-haired man.

She *would* tell him—maybe—but with Grammy's warning still ringing in her head, she wanted to check her grandmother's house herself, make sure there were no family secrets she didn't want revealed, because she was now convinced there *were* family secrets. She only hoped her family hadn't done anything illegal, which was why she wanted to visit Grammy's house by herself. Her grandmother had several guns. Abby would avail herself of one and Bates would be by her side. She should be safe enough.

But first she had to get rid of Noah.

TEN

There were two motels in Mocksville. Abby stayed quiet as Noah picked the one that fit his requirements for security. She had to admit the place was well lit and the clientele appeared to be of the family variety. She kept her mouth shut while they stood at the front desk and Noah requested rooms at the side of the building facing the street versus the back. But she did become vocal when he requested one room.

"I'm not spending the night with a man I'm not married to! It's not right and my grandmother would have a heart attack."

She assumed Noah would insist, but after rubbing his right temple, he ordered two rooms with an inner connecting door. Well, she'd lock the door between them. She meant what she'd said about not sharing a room, but she also planned on sneaking out after he was asleep.

She had to see what was in Grammy's house. Especially the attic, where old family belongings had been stored. She wanted to do it alone, but she wasn't foolish. She would take every precaution. She'd call a cab and have it drop her off at the house. She'd open the front door and let Bates check the place before she went inside. Then she'd go straight to her grandmother's bedroom and grab the gun hidden in the closet. Abby briefly wondered why her grandmother hadn't retrieved her gun. Maybe the intruders had surprised her and there wasn't time. Or had she known the intruder and allowed them in, not knowing what would happen? So many questions and very few answers. Abby was determined to find the answers tonight, after Noah was asleep.

He stopped in front of room number 122, first floor, facing the street, as requested. "It would have been safer at a hotel with rooms inside versus facing the outside," he grumbled.

Exasperated, Abby shot back, "At least we have two motels in Mocksville. Not so long ago there wasn't even one. We'll be fine here and Bates will be in my room. Trust me, I'll yell if anything happens." He smiled and guilt rode Abby hard. She was about to break an unspoken trust, but she didn't have any choice.

"I'm sure you will, and I enjoyed the local diner. Food was good," he admitted.

Noah preceded her into the room, gave it a once-over and unlocked the adjoining door. He shot her a suspicious look as he stood on the threshold, so she had to convince him he could trust her.

"Don't worry. Now that I think about it, you were right. It wouldn't have been safe staying at Grammy's. Let's get a good night's sleep and start fresh first thing in the morning. I appreciate your stopping at the grocery store. Bates wouldn't have been a happy camper without his dinner."

He hesitated, as if he wanted to say something, but only gave her a curt nod before closing the door.

Abby released the breath she'd been holding, tiptoed to the door and pressed her ear against the painted surface. She couldn't hear a thing, but just in case he could, she turned and faced Bates. "Come on, boy, I know you're hungry. Let's get you fed and then we're hitting the sack," she said in an overloud voice.

She fed and watered Bates, then stomped around the room as if preparing for bed. After thirty minutes, she lay down on the bed, fully clothed, turned off the lights and waited.

Abby Mayfield was up to something. But what? His gut told him it wouldn't take long to find out. She'd given in too easily when he insisted they stay at a hotel, and her little routine about being tired and ready to go to bed didn't ring true.

The only way she could leave without him was in the rental car he'd had delivered to the hospital or in a cab— if they had cabs in this small town. He'd made sure she didn't have access to the spare set of keys to the rental, so a cab was the logical solution. With a quick glance at his room, he kept his duffle bag in hand and eased out the door. Fall had brought a whiff of cool air, but it was warm enough to stay in the rental car where he could keep a watch for any intruders—and Ms. May-field herself.

He flung his duffle in the back, slid into the driver's seat and hunkered down to wait.

He passed the next hour thinking about everything that had transpired, but nothing made sense. He called his grandfather. Houston assured him Dylan was fine and asked all kinds of questions about Bates. Noah laughed when his granddad admitted to having to get on one of those stupid computers to find out more about the breed. Houston was from the old school. He and new technology didn't rub along very well. Noah didn't know what to think when his grandfather slyly told him that Dylan was asking a lot of questions about the new choir director in town. Like if she was married. They said goodbye and Noah hung up.

His phone vibrated and he checked caller ID.

"Coop, what's up?"

Cooper's voice quivered with excitement. "Sheriff, I took a notion to follow Walter Fleming and you'll never guess what I saw. I caught him meeting up with Joanne Ferguson. But that's not the best part. They didn't meet in the diner or any place like normal people. They met in the park. At night. As if they didn't want to be seen."

Interesting. There might be nothing to it, but... "Good work, Coop. And you're sure they didn't see you?"

"No, sir. I parked my car and followed on foot, but I didn't get close enough to hear anything. And there's more. Appeared to me like they were fighting. When they left, I followed Walter Fleming home. He went inside for about an hour, then came out the front door with a suitcase in hand. He got in his car and left."

A few threads started connecting and Noah straightened in his seat.

"What time did this happen yesterday?"

"Well, now that I think about it, it wasn't long after you and Ms. Mayfield left."

Noah got the tingly feeling he always got when things started coming together. It was almost too much to hope for. "Coop, did you keep following him?"

"I sure did. Straight to the airport."

Was it possible Walter Fleming had left his sedan at the Charlotte airport in North Carolina and rented a car in Texas?

"You did a great job. I'll be sure and tell your dad how well you're working out as deputy."

Cooper perked up. "Thanks, Sheriff. I'll keep tailing Joanne Ferguson and let you know if anything unusual happens."

"Sounds like a plan." A taxi pulled in to the parking lot and stopped in front of Abby's door. "Gotta go. Stay in touch."

He ended the call, slid down in his seat and watched Abby stealthily leave her room. She glanced around the parking lot, as if expecting him to jump out and stop her, then hurried to the cab. Before following her into the vehicle, Bates stopped, looked straight at Noah and perked his ears, then jumped in behind her.

Smart dog. Bates had spotted Noah, but didn't alert Abby. Noah decided Bates could play with Dylan anytime he wanted.

He waited until the cab pulled in to the deserted street—small towns closed down early—and followed. He had to ferret out Abby's secrets. Things were beginning to break loose and the call of the hunt soared through his veins.

Abby tried to control her rapid breathing as the cab approached Grammy's house. The closer they came to the neighborhood, the more Abby wondered if she had made a huge mistake by leaving Noah behind. There were people out there who wanted her dead, but she took a deep breath and calmed herself. She had to go through the attic without Noah. If she found anything about her parents that would hurt her grandmother—like family illegal activity—Abby would destroy it. She would protect her grandmother with her dying breath.

Why else would Grammy warn her not to trust anyone? Now that she knew her parents' names were possible aliases, Abby's imagination had run wild, and deep inside she knew something wasn't right.

Hopefully she would find answers in the attic where her grandmother had stored a ton of stuff. Grammy didn't have a safe-deposit box, and this was the only place Abby knew of to search for answers from the past. Bates nudged her hand with his cold nose after she paid the taxi, got the driver's number so she could call him back and stood alone in the darkness, facing the house she'd grown up in from the time she was six.

Once warm and welcoming, the house now looked cold and deserted with yellow police tape strung across the front. The porch light—always left on at night—was dark. Shoring up her courage, Abby ducked under the yellow tape and climbed the front steps. This might be her only chance to find answers and nothing was going to stop her. She removed a hidden key from the top of the door frame. Holding her breath, she unlocked the door. Nothing happened and she started breathing again.

"Okay, Bates, baby, check for bad guys."

The dog shot through the door and she shivered. She jumped when a neighborhood dog howled in the distance. She straightened her shoulders and took a deep breath when Bates came flying back out the front door, giving the all clear.

Hurrying in, she locked the door behind her and turned the dead bolt. Feeling a small measure of relief, she hit the light switch and gasped. The living room—to the right of the small foyer—was in shambles. Furniture was overturned and shattered lamps were scattered across the floor. Visions of her grandmother fighting for her life created a maelstrom of fury Abby had never before experienced.

"Lord, I'm asking You to remove my anger and help me find something that will lead us to the culprits."

Peace didn't steal over her—she was too livid for that—but she did calm down. She wanted this over as soon as possible. She refused to bring Grammy back here when she left the hospital. Abby would take her straight to Texas after this mess was resolved so they could start over.

"Come on, boy, let's see what we can find." After retrieving the gun, Abby felt bolder and pulled down the attic stairs using the attached string. She mounted the steps with Bates right behind her. When she reached the top, she flipped the light switch on the wall next to her and glanced around. Stuff was scattered everywhere. Old furniture covered with sheets. A bunch of boxes taped shut were piled high in one corner, as were all of Abby's baby things, which her grandmother had retrieved from her parents' house after they died.

Her parents. Were they even her parents? No! Abby wouldn't question that. Grammy would have told her something that life altering. Wouldn't she? Full of doubts about her very existence, Abby straightened her shoulders. "Okay, Bates, let's get started. We have to hurry if we want to get back to the motel before Noah wakes up." She moved across the creaky floor and lifted a dusty box off the top of the stack.

Surely there were papers, or something, that would explain the truth about her parentage. Was Grammy even her true grandmother? The mere thought was mind-blowing.

* * *

Noah shook his head at the rickety stairs he presumed led to the attic. Abby could have fallen and broken her neck, but this proved the woman had secrets.

Earlier, he had followed her from the motel and parked several houses down while the cabdriver deposited her in front of her grandmother's house. A mixture of admiration and irritation had vied for position as he'd watched her hesitate, then straighten her shoulders and march up the front steps.

The woman was gutsy. He couldn't fault her for not trusting him because he didn't fully trust *her*. There was something building between them that was more than mere attraction, but the woman was trouble. He didn't know if he wanted to deal with that.

He followed Abby's voice up the stairs. She spoke to her dog like he was a person.

There must be something hidden in the attic. Testing each step, he moved slowly up the stairs. He didn't want to scare her, but he did want to find out what she was hiding.

Noah quietly opened the door to the attic and watched as Abby lingered on a few of the treasures she'd unearthed from the boxes. It looked like she had a picture in her hand. He still couldn't believe she'd tried to give him the slip.

She made a small noise when she pulled something from the bottom of a box. She carefully unwrapped the tissue and lifted what looked like a pleated, vellum, silk-embroidered fan in front of her. She flicked her wrist and held the fan close to her face. Noah almost smiled when she spoke to her dog. "Well, Bates, do I look intriguing?"

The dog canted his head and stared at her.

"I'll take that as a yes." She lowered the fan and studied what he assumed were initials in the corner. "A.C. I remember Grammy saying the fan was passed down through Dad's family. I wonder if the *A* stands for Abigail. Maybe I was named after an ancestor. And who is that man who keeps popping up? And why did he allow me to see his face at the hospital?"

It was time to make his presence known. "I'd like the answers to both those questions."

His deep voice echoed from the top of the stairs, and even though he didn't want to scare her, he was almost glad to see her jump. She needed to know anyone could have followed her and broken into the house, just like he had. She could be dead right now if that had happened. From her position on the floor, she glanced over her shoulder and met his gaze. The jig was up, but righteous indignation set in and she went on the offense.

"You're not my keeper and I don't have to tell you anything. I have enough sense to protect myself." Reaching to the floor beside her, she lifted the Glock. "I have Bates and I'm locked and loaded."

Noah took long strides across the wide, wooden planks and sat on the floor beside her. He relieved her of the gun and released a long breath. It was time to be honest with himself. The woman was driving him crazy, and in more ways than one.

He hadn't dated since Sonya had passed away two years ago because that felt as if it would be unfaithful to his dead wife. Then Ms. Abigail—Abby—blew into his life like a hurricane, catching him off guard. Maybe it was time to join the land of the living again. If only he could trust her.

He turned his head and gazed at her soft brown eyes. He had no idea how she felt about him, and that made him edgy. He didn't like feeling unsure about anything. He'd been told he had nerves of steel, but they seemed to have deserted him.

"Noah? Is something wrong?"

"Yes! I'm attracted to you." His face heated and he scrambled to his feet. He couldn't believe he'd just blurted it out like that. He was an idiot. "I can't believe I just said that."

Her eyes softened, and she stood up and faced him. He wanted to fall through the floor when she grinned.

"So that's what's wrong? You're attracted to me?"

"No. I mean yes. I don't know what I mean. Forget I said anything."

She moved close and cupped his cheek with one hand. "It's okay. I'm kinda attracted to you, too."

Before he could stop himself, he pressed his lips softly to hers and she relaxed against his chest. Noah thought of a million reasons he shouldn't be doing this—one being he was supposed to be protecting her—but it felt so right.

After the sweetest kiss, he pulled back and tucked a stray strand of hair behind her ear. "You're the most beautiful, exasperating, kindhearted, troublesome woman I've ever met."

She opened her mouth, probably to take exception to his words, but he placed a finger on her lips.

"Abby, you have to trust me. Your life is in danger and we have to work together. There can be no secrets. If you have information, you have to share."

With no warning, she jerked out of his arms. "You just kissed me to try to butter me up. I don't appreciate that."

Horror filled his mind. "You're wrong. Everything I said is true. I think you're a wonderful person."

He could almost hear her brain going a hundred miles an hour.

"Why don't we agree to table this discussion until later?" She took a deep breath. "And you're right. I do have to trust someone." She picked up the fan. "While going through some old boxes, I came across this fan. When I was a child, I remember Grammy saying it had been passed down through our family." She pointed at the initials. "I'm wondering if the *A* stands for Abigail, maybe a name that's been passed down through the generations. I don't know what the *C* would stand for."

Noah wanted to disagree with her about discussing the kiss later, but he moved on. "I'm more interested in the man at the hospital."

She hesitated, then shrugged. "I'll tell you, but I want your word that if we find something incriminating about my family, anything that would hurt Grammy, you won't tell anyone."

His mouth formed a tight line. "I can't promise you that."

She appeared to mull it over and he breathed a sigh of relief when she said, "Fine. I'm pretty sure the man I saw at the hospital is the same one I spotted standing in the woods at the car crash."

"Describe what he looked like and his demeanor toward you. Did he appear hostile?"

Bates plopped down beside her and she ran a hand over his soft fur. "No," she said slowly. "He had a wistful expression on his face. It was odd, but I didn't feel threatened."

"Did you get a good enough look at his face to work with a police sketch artist?"

"Yes, I did."

"I'll set that up, and I have some information that

might tie into this. Cooper called. He followed Walter Fleming. Fleming left town shortly after we did."

"You think Walter ran us off the road?" She blew out a breath. "I still don't believe one of my choir members is involved in this. What about Joanne Ferguson?"

"Coop is keeping a close eye on her."

Abby excitedly waved the fan in front of her. "The fan. Look at the initials."

He took the fan and squinted at the small print. "You said they were A.C."

Abby bounced on the floor. "Yes! The fan and the license plate you saw before we went over the embankment both have *C*. This could be our first clue."

"That's quite a long shot. Most license plates are random."

She shook her head. "True, but a lot of people have personalized plates. It's worth looking into."

Bates lifted his head, ears pricked. He stood on all fours and whined.

Noah frowned.

"What?" Abby whispered.

"Shh. Give me a second."

He strained to hear what had caused the dog's reaction and heard a faint ticking sound. Noah grabbed Abby's arm and pulled her to her feet. Bates started growling.

"Get out! Now! Go, go, go."

"What is it?" she shouted.

"It's a bomb. Run!"

ELEVEN

Abby froze and Noah pulled her across the planked floor. "Wait! The family pictures. We might need them."

He pushed her toward the stairs. "Go! Follow Bates. I'll grab what I can and be right behind you."

Even with fear tightening her throat and making it hard to breathe, Abby followed Bates down the rickety stairs. In the midst of a possible bomb destroying Grammy's house, it still amazed her that a dog could be trained to climb and descend stairs.

She hit the bottom step and turned, waiting for Noah to come scrambling down behind her. When he didn't appear, she yelled at the top of her lungs. The pictures weren't worth his life. "Noah, leave the boxes. Get down here."

She blew out the breath she'd been holding when he made an appearance at the top of the stairs.

"Get out! I'm coming," he yelled.

She turned to run. Bates flew out the front door. She had one foot over the threshold when an earsplitting explosion rocked her world. As if in a dream, her body lifted into the air before a bone-jarring slam claimed the breath in her lungs.

A thick cloud of smoke followed the boom. Barely

conscious, her eyes watered. She coughed and tried to draw air into her lungs. "Bates," she whispered, relieved when a wet tongue licked her face.

"Bates. Find Noah." She fought the darkness closing in. Noah had been right behind her. Did the explosion kill him? She rolled to her side and tried to stand. Bates growled and a voice penetrated the pain and dizziness overtaking her.

"It's okay, boy. Take a big sniff." A hand found her shoulder and gently pushed her back down. "Shh, it'll be okay. I called 911."

Abby fought the smoke-induced tears and stared at the man. "It's you," she breathed. "The man in the woods and at the hospital. Who are you?" She inhaled a lungful of smoke and coughed. Noah! Right now it didn't matter who the guy was, he had to help Noah. "Noah. He's still inside. Please help him." Abby fought as long as she could, but the throbbing in her head won the battle and she reluctantly closed her eyes, giving in to the darkness.

Noah hadn't prayed in years, but he'd sent up a heart-felt one. "God, please get her to safety." As the words had left his mouth, a deafening boom had filled the old house and the stairs gave way. He'd been halfway down and fell to the floor as hot embers burned through his shirt and pierced his skin.

He'd rolled when he hit the floor, taking the brunt of the fall on his left shoulder. Scrambling to his feet, he'd grabbed the box of pictures that had fallen to the floor, and would have made it out if the ceiling hadn't caved. Now, through the roar of the fire, he heard Bates barking and it terrified him. This whole thing could have been planned, with people waiting outside, ready to kill

Abby if the fire didn't do its job. But how would anyone guess that Abby would show up at her grandmother's house tonight? It had been a spur-of-the-moment decision.

A falling beam knocked him sideways and landed on his left leg, effectively trapping him in the roaring fire. He tried to push the wood off and pull his leg loose, but it would take the help of another person to free him.

Gritting his teeth as debris and hot embers rained down on him, scorching his skin, he grabbed a chunk of wood that had fallen from the ceiling. It was hot, but he forced the wood under the beam and shoved with all his might. It didn't budge an inch.

Giving up was not an option. Noah had a son to raise and he refused to leave Dylan orphaned. He coughed and took shallow breaths, trying to stay alive long enough to figure a way out of the situation.

Through the dense smoke, he saw movement and called out. There hadn't been time for the fire department to arrive. Maybe a neighbor? Or the people trying to hurt Abby? Locking his jaw, he lifted his midsection and reached back, relieved to find his gun still in the waistband of his jeans. He pointed and cocked the weapon just as a man appeared in the smoke. The crazy guy ignored the gun and rushed over to Noah. Bates belly crawled in behind him, grabbed Noah's pant leg and started pulling.

"Put the gun away. I'm here to help," the man choked out.

Noah didn't have much choice. The stranger took the piece of wood out of his hand and placed the tip under the beam.

"On the count of three," he yelled.

Noah nodded.

"One, two, three!"

Noah scooted back on his hands, grabbed the box of pictures laying on the floor beside him and crawled to all fours before forcing himself to his feet. His leg burned like fire, but it wasn't broken. He was mobile. Barely.

The person threw his arm around Noah's waist and pulled him forward.

"Go, go, go. The roof's gonna cave."

Noah propelled himself forward. They made it to the front porch, and he thought they were home free until the roof collapsed and a sharp object pierced his temple. Black dots blurred his vision, but the guy kept pulling him forward and lowered him to ground when they were clear of the fire. Taking a deep breath of clean air, Noah tried to get a visual on the man leaning over him. His face was slightly blurred.

"Hey, you're okay, and so is Abby."

Noah had a million questions, the first being how this person knew Abby's name, but a coughing fit halted all inquiries. He had blond hair. Could it be the same man from the crash scene and the hospital?

Noah heard a siren wailing in the distance and the man leaned closer.

"Listen, I know who you are, ex-FBI agent Noah Galloway and I know your history. Abby and her grandmother need to disappear and you can make that happen. Please, I beg you, use your contacts and help her."

The sirens were getting closer.

"I gotta go."

Noah lifted his hand to stop the man, but it fell to his side, weakened by his injuries.

* * *

The sound of a soft beep gently woke Abby and her eyes popped open. She was in a hospital. Memories of the explosion at her grandmother's house rushed into her brain. She briefly closed her lids against the pounding in her head.

Noah! Bates!

She tried to move herself into a sitting position, but was gently pushed back down by a woman wearing a nurse's uniform.

"You're in the hospital, but you're okay. A little smoke inhalation and a few bumps and bruises, but no serious injuries." The woman was being nice, but Abby had a searing desire to see Noah and Bates and make sure they were okay.

"I don't care about me. Where are Noah and Bates?"

A whine came from the side of the bed and Abby turned her head. Relieved, she stretched out her arm and touched Bates on the nose. "You okay, boy?"

A throat cleared. Sheriff Brady moved in beside her dog and frowned. "The animal wouldn't allow anyone in the hospital to touch you unless he was by your side. He's created chaos in this building. I almost called animal control."

Fury tore through Abby, but she contained her anger and gritted her teeth. "Where is Noah?"

The sheriff snorted. "You're just like your grandmother. All sweet Southern charm on the outside, the disposition of a wildcat on the inside. I didn't call animal control because the dog likely saved Noah's life. We found teeth marks on his jeans."

He held up a hand when she tried to interrupt. "I know we'll never be best friends, but I'm here to help in any way I can. Noah's fine. Same as you, smoke inhalation, bumps and bruises, a few minor burns and a nasty bruise on his leg. I'm sure he'll be along shortly. He refused treatment until the doctor threatened to stick a needle in him and put him to sleep unless he got checked. I'll warn you, he does have a nasty wound on his temple, but the doc assured him it wasn't a concussion. Y'all were blessed to come out of that mess alive."

He scraped a chair across the floor and sat down next to her bed. "I'm sure you realize I have a ton of questions. We have some major problems on our hands."

Abby whipped her head around when a deep, scratchy voice came from the vicinity of the doorway. "We appreciate all your help, Sheriff, but as soon as Abby is up to it, we're headed to New York. I have contacts there who can hopefully help us find some answers."

At the sight of him, Abby's heart pounded in her chest. Noah had a bandage on his temple, his shirt had small burn holes in it and his jeans were torn. He looked like he'd just been in a war zone. And that's what her life felt like. A war zone.

How had this happened? She was a simple choir director who'd never harmed anyone in her life.

"I need to talk to Abby alone," Noah said to the sheriff.

The sheriff stood. "Fine, I'll need a statement, for all the good it'll do. From what the fire chief concluded after the first walk-through, it was a professional job. I don't think the answers lie in my county."

Noah didn't respond and the sheriff left. Abby stared at Noah, drinking him in. He moved to the side of her bed. He looked like he wanted to touch her, and Abby couldn't decide if she was happy or sad that he didn't.

"That was a close call, Abby. We have to find answers fast."

She swallowed hard, knowing what she had to do. "Noah." Her voice cracked and she tried again. "Noah, you have a son to raise. Whatever's going on is too dangerous. I can't allow you to risk your life. We don't even know who these people are."

He gave her a lopsided grin and it lifted her heart. "I appreciate the sentiment, and I don't plan on leaving Dylan orphaned, but this is what I do."

Her heart fell. Even though he was ready to risk his life to save hers, this was exactly why she should distance herself from that kiss in her grandmother's attic and whatever was happening between them. Determined, she thrust out her chin. She might not be able to convince him to change his mind, but there was one thing she could do.

"If anything happens to you, I'll take care of Dylan. I promise."

He grinned and his electric-blue eyes twinkled. "That won't happen, but Dylan would love having Bates full time."

They both chuckled at his lame attempt at breaking the tension.

He sat in the chair beside the bed and his smile melted away. "Are you up to talking about the explosion? But before we start, I checked on your grandmother. Her condition is stable, but they're still keeping her in an induced coma for the time being."

"I appreciate that, and I do want to discuss anything that will help us understand this mess."

He leaned back in his chair, as if contemplating what to say. "A man, at high risk to himself, ran into that burning house and saved my life. My leg was trapped under a beam and he helped free me. He pulled me out of the house with the front porch roof collapsing on top of us."

Abby's heart beat faster. "He has blond hair."

Noah nodded. "So you saw him?"

"Yes! He was the same man at the crash site and the hospital. He made sure I was okay and I told him you were still in the house."

Noah nodded as if he'd figured as much. "The question is…why was he there in the first place? And who is he? If he's working for the bad guys, it was a perfect time to kill us."

Abby felt the blood rush from her brain and Noah stood when she swayed. "You're not okay. I'm calling the nurse."

She waved a hand in the air. "I'm fine. It's not every day a girl has a close brush with death. Just give me a minute." She took several deep breaths. "So, who do you think he is?"

"I have no clue, but don't worry. We'll find out."

Noah hesitated and Abby jumped all over it. "You're hiding something. What is it?"

"The blond man made a good suggestion. He asked me to hide you and your grandmother. Permanently."

Abby shook her head fiercely. "You can get that right out of your mind, Noah Galloway. I won't rest until the people who hurt my grandmother are behind bars."

Noah shrugged. "I figured that's what you'd say. Okay, then, Coop called. Joanne Ferguson left Blessing. It wouldn't surprise me if she's headed to North Carolina, but we won't be here. Alex Ridenhour, my old partner from the FBI, called. Simon, our resident computer whiz, found out that both Joanne Ferguson and Walter Fleming aren't who they claim to be. They passed a surface search, but Simon dug deeper, and their false identities didn't hold up."

"Do you think Walter Fleming tried to blow us up?"

"Like I said, we'll find out. We're starting to connect the dots. Simon is working on the car tag. He's already eliminated half the list of plates starting with *C-A-M*. It's only a matter of time before we have a name to go with the tag, unless the plates were stolen."

Abby groaned. "It can't ever be easy, can it?" Then she cheered up. "But God never said it was going to be easy, did he?"

Noah ignored the biblical reference. "Let's get you out of here and go track down some bad guys."

TWELVE

A nurse took Abby out of the hospital in a wheelchair and she fussed all the way to the car Noah left idling beside the curb, claiming she had two good legs and could walk perfectly well. Noah bit back a grin when the nurse muttered "Good riddance" under her breath after helping Abby up and into the vehicle.

Noah rounded the hood, slid into the driver's seat and grinned at her. "We look like a couple of refugees." They both chuckled, but he was concerned about her health. "You sure you're up to this? You can always stay with your grandmother. Sheriff Brady posted a guard on her door 24/7. You'd be safe here."

She puckered her lips, a telling sign of irritation. "No. Grammy is being well taken care of, and—" her lips tightened "—I have to see this through. If my grandmother taught me anything, it's to face my fears head-on." Her voice firmed and a dangerous glint entered her eyes. "And when we find the person who hurt her, I have a couple of things I'd like to say to them."

Noah grinned and put the car in Drive. "I just bet you do. We'll swing by the motel, change clothes and grab our bags."

After a quick shower and change of clothes, Noah felt

like a human being again. His throat was sore and his body ached, but that was to be expected. He shuddered every time he thought about their brush with death and how close Abby had come to dying.

They'd been in the rental car for thirty minutes. Neither of them had spoken, but it was a relaxed, comfortable silence. His fingers were wrapped loosely around the steering wheel. He quickly glanced at Abby as she stared at the passing scenery out the passenger window, then turned his gaze back to the road. She had dressed in black leggings and a loose top that came to her thighs. She'd pulled her soft-looking blond hair up into a ponytail.

"So, you grew up in Texas?" she asked without turning her head.

The question made him uneasy. He never talked about his past if he could avoid it. His fingers tightened on the steering wheel for a moment before he forced them to relax.

"Yep. I grew up there, went to college and joined the FBI."

Out of the corner of his eye, he saw Abby fiddle with a loose string on the bottom of her sweater. "That's it? Sounds to me as if you left out a lot of stuff. If you don't want to talk about it, that's fine with me."

A new, tense silence filled the car and it irritated him.

"Why did you kiss me in the attic?"

The question came out of left field and his body tensed, but then he blew out a breath and chuckled. "You're one tough cookie, Abby Mayfield."

The tension leaked out of the car and she grinned. "You betcha."

He took a moment, gathering his thoughts. "I kissed

you because it felt right, not to get information. And as for my childhood… Well, let's just say my family would never be nominated for a family of the year award."

Abby lifted a questioning brow and he shrugged. He'd kissed the woman, which he figured gave her the right to delve into his dysfunctional past.

"My mom skipped out when I was ten. My old man was sheriff, but he was also a mean drunk."

Her expression softened and she reached across the console to touch his arm. "Noah, I'm sorry. I shouldn't have intruded into your personal life. You don't have to talk about it if you don't want to."

Her offer sounded genuine and he relaxed. "No, I want to tell you." He paused and took a deep breath, preparing to open old wounds. "I don't blame my mother for leaving. My dad was sheriff, but he lived on the shady side of life. He traded favors with people and made deals he shouldn't have."

"Your mother left her child with a drunk father of questionable character?"

Her indignation and protectiveness on his behalf warmed him. Grandpa Houston had raised him, for the most part, but his grandfather wasn't exactly what you'd call soft and fuzzy. Houston had spent Noah's childhood teaching Noah how to be a man. And working on a ranch part-time wasn't conducive to much coddling.

"Not exactly, but when you live in a small town and your old man's the sheriff, let's just say she didn't have a fighting chance of taking me with her."

"Have you stayed in touch with her?"

"When I got older, I tracked her down. She remarried and has two daughters. She deserves to be happy."

"What about now? I was there when your father called, asking to see Dylan."

His grip tightened on the steering wheel and his knuckles turned white. "He claims to be on the wagon, but I've heard that too many times to count. He doesn't deserve to see my son. I don't trust him." He paused. "But there was a silver lining in my childhood."

"What was that?" she asked.

His gave her a genuine smile. "Grandpa Houston. He's a wily old coot."

Abby laughed. "He's a sweet man with a wonderful, deep baritone voice. I think he should join the choir."

A hoarse laugh escaped before Noah could stop it. "I'd like to see that. Grandpa's smart as a whip. I spent the majority of my childhood on his ranch, learning all the ropes. It helped make up for the time spent at home with dear old Pop."

"You grew up a cowboy, joined the FBI and now you're a sheriff. Some people would call you an overachiever."

Bates blew out a sigh from the back seat and they both laughed.

"Turnabout's fair play. I know about your grandmother and your parents. Did you have a good childhood?"

Abby turned introspective. "The loss of my parents was devastating, but Grammy made up for it. I had a wonderful childhood, except…"

"Except?" he prodded.

"I would have loved to have had a brother or sister."

"I know what you mean. I have two half sisters, but I've never met them."

"Maybe it's time you did."

"What?" The thought startled him. After tracking down his mother, he'd thought it best to leave her and her new family in peace. He didn't think she would enjoy having a grown son show up unannounced on her doorstep. She'd probably shaken the Texas dust from her feet and hadn't looked back.

"Maybe it's time you met your sisters. As we've recently learned, life can be short. I'm sure they'd love to have a big brother looking out for them."

It was an intriguing idea. "I just might do that."

His phone buzzed and Abby turned back to gazing out her window, but he knew she was listening to his conversation. She glanced at him when Dylan's name came up.

"Hey, Dylan, what's up, son? Grandpa Houston treating you right?...Chocolate chip cookies?" He smiled. "That's great. I'm with Ms. Mayfield and we're driving to New York...Yep, we're tracking down the people who broke into her house, but you don't need to worry, we'll find them and put them in a nice, cozy cell...Yes, Bates is with us."

Noah cleared his throat and lowered his voice. "We can discuss that when I get back home...Not now, we'll discuss it first." Noah released a big sigh and handed Abby the phone. "He wants to talk to you."

Abby took the phone and grinned. She loved kids and their cute antics. "Hey, Dylan. Did you want to speak to me?"

"Yes, ma'am. Is my dad doing okay?"

"Yes. He's just fine. Why do you ask?"

"Well, sometimes he works too hard and I don't think he has enough fun. When y'all get back, maybe we can go on a picnic or something."

Abby choked back a laugh. The kid was playing matchmaker for his father. It was funny but serious, too. She had to be careful with Dylan because she didn't know if she was ready for a relationship with any man, much less one with a dangerous profession, even though she'd love to have a smart, cheerful child like Dylan brightening up her life.

"That's a good suggestion. We'll discuss it when things settle down."

"I'd like to be in the church Christmas play, and maybe it'd be a good idea if I started taking piano lessons, too."

Dear Lord, have mercy on this sweet child, was the first thing to pop into Abby's mind. She had taught children long enough to know when she was being manipulated, and she also knew how to handle it.

"Now, Dylan, you know I'd love to have you in the Christmas play and as a piano student, but don't you think your father should have a say in this? And you need to ask yourself why you want to take piano lessons. Is it a lifelong dream of yours, something you're willing to give up other after-school activities for?"

Dead silence filled the phone, then he said, "Maybe not the piano lessons, but I definitely want to be in the Christmas play."

"And I'd love to have you, after you discuss it with your father."

"Can I talk to him again?"

"Certainly." Abby handed the phone back to Noah. He mouthed "Thank you" and took the phone.

Her mind wandered while he finished his call. Her life had been turned upside down, but Noah's soft tones and loving conversation with his son filled her with longing. She was twenty-eight years old and had always wanted a family with two or three children hanging on to her skirts, as her grandmother would say.

Thinking of Grammy brought the ugly reality of

her life crashing back in. She glanced at Noah and the soft, sweet look on his face as he spoke with Dylan gave her heart a jolt. So what if he worked in a dangerous environment, her heart argued. Her deceased husband had led the safest life any wife could ask for, yet it had been cut short by a car crash. A dark, unsettling thought crossed her mind as Noah hung up the phone.

"That son of mine is a pistol..." His words trailed off when he caught her expression. "What? What's wrong?"

Abby tried to shake off the ugly thought, but it wouldn't budge. Once there, it took hold and expanded. *God, are You sending me a message?*

"What if..."

"What if what?"

"What if my husband's and parents' deaths weren't accidents? They were all killed in car crashes. Don't you think that's odd? The three people closest to me died in car accidents?"

Noah didn't laugh. She appreciated that he took her conspiracy theory seriously.

"I think," he said slowly, "that we'll stop by my old office in New York before we do anything else. I have lots of connections. If your theory is right, we'll need some help, but it's really a long shot. There's too many years between the accidents. It doesn't make any sense. Why would the perpetrator wait so long between murders? There's no motive that we know of."

She nodded, then remembered something. The boxes of pictures Noah had risked his life for. She cringed at the thought. If he had died during the explosion at her grandmother's house, his blood would have been on her hands. Pushing the morbid thought away, she reached behind her seat, grabbed the box and plopped it across her thighs.

Noah glanced at her lap. She grinned at his raised eyebrows when he spotted Grammy's Glock in the box on top of the pictures. The ambulance attendants had rescued the box on the ground beside Noah after the explosion, and it was given to Abby in the hospital. Thankfully no one had looked inside. "A girl's gotta have protection. And I haven't thanked you for saving both the pictures and Grammy's gun. It's amazing that you were able to get both out of the house after the explosion. I didn't take any pictures with me to Texas because I'd planned to move Grammy as soon as it was safe. I was going to go through everything in her attic at that time."

He didn't say a word and she started digging through the pictures. They brought back a lot of memories. Some sad, but mostly good.

She held up one of the photos. "I begged to go to Disney World for over a year. On Christmas morning, I opened a present and there were the tickets." A tear slid down her cheek. "It was a wonderful trip."

"You don't have to do this right now."

She gripped his strong fingers. "Yes, I do. There might be a clue buried in these pictures. I haven't thanked you for saving them from the fire."

"You're welcome." He grinned. "You were a cute girl."

"And you, Noah Galloway, are a kind liar. I was a chubby kid, but I do have to say I grew out of it when I was about ten. My baby fat just disappeared."

His lips stretched into a big grin and he chuckled. "I'd love to have a cute, chubby baby daughter that looked just like her mama." His grin was replaced by an expression of horror. "I didn't mean…"

She laughed. She hadn't seen Noah at a loss for

words since meeting him. He was so in control all the time, it was a relief to see he was human, after all.

"No worries. I didn't take it as a proposal."

They both laughed and Abby absently picked another picture out of the box. Her amusement died, her heart lurched, and frustration took hold.

"What is it?"

She held the picture up where he could see it. "It's another picture of my parents holding that same baby." She scrutinized the background. "I don't remember ever seeing this one. They appear to be at a fair or carnival of some sort. I can't make out any identifying marks or names."

"Keep it out. We'll take it with us to the FBI and see if Simon can find anything."

Her stomach lurched and nausea followed. She could explain away two pictures, but three? What were her parents doing with the same child in three pictures? Her original explanation was beginning to waver. Would they travel to that many places with another couple and have their pictures taken with the other couple's kid?

Dizziness blurred her vision when Noah asked, "Abby, sweetheart, are you sure you're an only child?"

THIRTEEN

Noah jerked the car off the side of the interstate after glancing at Abby. Her face had turned paper white. He slammed the car into Park and took her hand in his.

"Abby, I'm sorry. I shouldn't have said that."

She rolled her shoulders, as if shrugging off a heavy weight. "I'm okay, and you have nothing to be sorry for, but what if you're right? What if I have a sibling?"

He was coming to admire many things about her, especially her fortitude and strength.

"If what you said is true, my whole life is a lie and my parents were dishonest." She firmed her lips. "They took me to church every Sunday. What if we sat in that pew every week and their lives were full of deception?"

She looked frustrated and upset, and he didn't like that his careless words were the cause. "I'm just being silly. I'm sure there's a good explanation for the pictures."

Her eyes were full of hurt and questions. He was determined to give her the answers she desired, but something else in her expression bothered him.

"Abby, whatever we find out about your parents, you can't let it shake your faith."

She snorted and the small sign of normality lifted his spirits.

"This from a man who doesn't go to church anymore?"

He grinned. "Maybe times are changing," he joked.

She smiled and laid the picture back in the box. "There could be a million reasons why my parents had these pictures made, and as you cops like to say, I shouldn't assume anything without proof."

With things calm now, Noah pulled the rental car back onto the highway. "Absolutely true."

A comfortable silence filled the vehicle as Noah drove, his thoughts processing everything that had happened in such a short period of time. He also considered Abby's suggestion about meeting his half sisters. For so many years, he'd blamed his mother for leaving him, but did she really have a choice? Abby had a way of making him rethink his past and look at it from his mother's perspective.

He pulled in to a paid parking garage and tried to gently shake her awake. She had fallen asleep during the long ride. "We're here." She lifted a hand to fidget with her hair and he chuckled.

"Don't worry, you look fine."

She gave him a disgruntled look and fished a comb and compact out of her purse. She responded to his interested stare. "I refuse to meet your friends looking like something my dog dragged in."

He laughed and peered at her purse. "I always wondered what women toted around in those big pocketbooks."

She sliced him a sharp look. "That's none of your business, Noah Galloway."

He held his hands up in mock surrender, then turned

serious. "Listen, Abby, you've been through a lot. I can easily place you in a temporary safe house until this is over. Your grandmother is secure at the hospital in North Carolina. I'd prefer you to be protected, too."

Her jaw firmed resolutely. "I'm staying glued to your side until this mess is over. I want to know who's doing this and why. They've turned my life inside out and I want a word with them before they're hauled off to jail for the rest of their lives."

"And the steel magnolia makes an appearance," he muttered.

"I heard that."

"Okay, then, let's go."

Abby invited Bates out of the car and hooked a leash to his collar. They left the parking garage, emerged onto the street and headed toward the FBI building. "Wow," Abby breathed.

Noah guided her across the street. People gave them a wide berth when they noticed the dog.

"Impressive, isn't it?"

"I'll say. You really worked here? It's so different from Blessing."

He shot her a rueful look. "Like night and day."

Without warning, Abby tugged on his sleeve, pulling him to a stop on the sidewalk. "Noah, you said you moved to Blessing to protect Dylan because of the thing with the mayor. Is Dylan's life still in danger? Were all the bad guys caught and put in jail?"

Once again, her concern for him and his son warmed his heart. He explained the situation, hoping to put her mind at ease. "Jack Vitale—Big Jack—was killed during the investigation. We couldn't get enough evidence against his son, Anthony, to put him behind bars. He made a few threats, which is why I moved back to Blessing, but I believe they're empty threats. The FBI keeps close tabs on him and they'll notify me of any changes."

"That's why you leave Dylan with your grandfather when you're gone."

"Dylan is safe on the ranch. There are plenty of ranch hands milling about at any given time, and all of them would spot a stranger a long way off. Plus, Grandpa Houston knows how to shoot a gun, and he won't hesitate to use it if need be. Come on, let's go inside."

Noah led the way and Abby followed him through the front doors. They had to go through security, and she threw him an endearing, embarrassed glance when she had to empty the contents of her purse into a container for security. He grinned at the amount of stuff she had, but knew better than to comment on the things a woman thought she needed to cart around everywhere. There were several questions and a few snafus about the dog, and then they were on their way.

An elevator took them to the twenty-third floor and they stepped into his comfortable past. The boisterous office was loud and filled with numerous cubicles. People ran to and fro all over the place. Many had phones glued to their ears and several stood in their cubicles, shouting across the room.

It felt like coming home, and he missed it, but Noah had no regrets. Blessing was a great place to raise Dylan, and he was starting to appreciate the peace and quiet more every day versus the hustle and bustle of New York. He was a country boy at heart.

An old friend walked down the aisle, looked up, grinned and shouted to the room at large. "Look what the cat dragged in. If it isn't Sheriff Galloway, returned to the big city."

The man slapped Noah on the back and a group of

men surrounded him, all talking at once. He was aware of Abby standing outside of the close-knit circle. Noah had always gotten along with most of his former co-workers.

Except one.

"And who have we here?"

Noah whipped around and moved to Abby's side. "Back off, Romeo. She's with me."

Noah gave the guy his due. He'd guess most women would consider him good-looking in his starched shirt and pressed jeans. He waggled his brows at Abby and Noah didn't like it.

All the men laughed.

"Stay away from him. He loves all women." Noah tried to make his comment sound humorous, but he didn't quite manage it through his clenched teeth.

Abby smiled and Noah took her hand. There was a round of Ho Hos before he sobered and put a stop to the silly nonsense.

"Abby's having a few problems and we need some help."

Like turning off a light switch, the men went from jovial to solemn in an instant. Every man there offered to help Noah in any way needed and Abby blinked back the moisture in her eyes. They were so nice. It was obvious Noah was well respected and well liked by his peers.

He pulled her through the group toward a large office at the back of the room. Through the glass walls she spotted two men, one seated behind a large desk and the other standing in front of it.

"Good. Just the people we need to see."

Bates picked up on Abby's anxiety and released a

low rumble. She rested her hand on his head as they followed Noah. "It's okay, baby. I'm just a tad nervous. No one in their right mind would want to visit an FBI office."

Noah must have overheard her. He shot her a quick grin over his shoulder before the two guys in the office greeted him with enthusiasm. It was interesting to see him in this environment.

With his notoriety in saving the mayor's life, she assumed a small amount of jealousy abounded in the office, too. She hoped she looked okay when Noah turned to introduce her.

"Abby, meet Director Henry Wilson, my old boss, and this crazy guy is my former partner, Alex Ridenhour."

Both men had firm, but non-ego-enhanced handshakes. Abby liked their smiles. "Nice to meet you, gentlemen. This guy beside me is Bates, my best friend and the greatest protection dog in the world."

Director Wilson grinned. "I hear a strong Southern accent, and, please, call me Henry."

"You're right. I was born and bred in North Carolina, south of the Mason–Dixon Line, and you may call me Abby."

Everyone in the room laughed and Noah's eyes lit with amusement. His twinkle of pleasure warmed her entire being.

The ice was broken and Henry got down to business. "Noah, Alex tells me the two of you have run into a few problems down in Texas."

Noah pulled a third chair in front of Henry's desk and the three of them sat down.

"Yes, sir. I called on Alex and Simon to help out with a few things, but our problems have become complicated and we need resources I don't have available in Texas. I don't have enough information to warrant bringing in the FBI, but—"

Henry interrupted and waved away Noah's concerns. "No problem. Tell me what's going on and how we can help."

Their smiles turned into grimaces as Noah explained their situation.

A frown creased the director's forehead and he turned his attention toward Abby. "You have no idea who may be doing this?"

Everyone stared at her, as if she should have the answers. "I'm sorry, I don't have any idea who's behind any of this, but I plan on finding out, no matter how long it takes or what I have to do." Anger laced her next words. "They hurt my grandmother."

Director Wilson's eyebrows rose at her forcefulness, but she'd had enough. It was time for action.

The director glanced at Noah and grinned. "I can see why you like it down there in Texas."

The men laughed, then went straight to the matter at hand.

"Alex, get Fisher on board. Let's see if we can get a picture of Fleming, Ferguson and the unknown man."

Noah explained. "Abby, Joe Fisher is the best sketch artist the FBI has on staff. If you can describe Joanne, Walter and the unknown man, he'll draw them and we'll run the pictures through our system, see if anything shows up. I'll also work with him on Fleming and our unknown, since I've seen both of them."

Director Wilson gave more orders to Alex. "Get Simon to examine the picture placed at the carnival. Maybe he can dig out a location where the shot was taken, and also see how he's coming with the partial plate number."

Abby nodded at Noah, dug the picture out of her purse and handed it to the director.

Noah cleared his throat and Director Wilson raised a questioning brow in his direction. "Abby insists on being involved in the investigation."

Noah's former boss sighed. "It's your responsibility and your call. You no longer work for the FBI."

Noah gave him a crooked grin. "Thanks. I appreciate the help."

Abby stood when Noah rose. He reached across the desk to shake Wilson's hand. "You have my cell number. I'll take Abby down to Joe's office."

Director Wilson grimaced at Abby. "Please accept my apologies in advance for the state of Joe's office. He's not the neatest person."

She nodded, but before she could follow Noah out of the director's office there was a quick knock and the door was slung wide-open. A young guy—he looked like he belonged in high school with his old sneakers, torn-at-the-knee jeans and ratty sweatshirt—practically ran them down as he rushed into the room. His eyes lit up when he spotted Noah.

"Noah! I heard you were in the building." He straightened his shoulders as he stood in front of them. "I've been good. I swear it." The kid glanced at Alex, and Abby smiled at his exuberance. "Tell him, Alex."

He jerked his gaze back toward Noah without waiting for Alex to answer. "I have straight As this semester and I haven't broken into any computers except when Director Wilson told me to."

Abby grinned at Noah and he chuckled. "Abby, this

is Simon, and I'll explain his role here at the FBI later," he whispered.

To Simon, he said, "That's good to hear. Did you track me down for a reason?"

It was then Simon noticed Abby standing to the side. He flushed an unbecoming red and stammered. "S-sorry, ma'am, I didn't see you there."

Noah took charge. "Simon!"

"Yes. I concentrated on the car and the plate beginning with the letters *C-A-M*. We're running them through the DMV, but I also connected my computer with every major traffic cam, including airport security cameras, to try to track the movement of car itself." In an aside, he said to Abby, "The terrorism threats make it easy for me to find stuff. We have cameras all over the place now."

She kept quiet and he continued, "I had Franny—that's my computer's name—run a cross-reference to see what plates crossed state lines in the last twelve months and where they went."

He beamed and Noah sighed. "And?"

"A beige sedan popped up at the Charlotte airport and on a street in New York, but there's a problem."

"And that is?" Noah asked patiently.

Simon studied the hole in his sneaker. "I got a clear visual on the letters—*C-A-M*—but it looked like someone smeared mud on the rest of the plate."

Abby's heart sank. Every time they took one step forward, if felt as if they took two steps back.

FOURTEEN

Abby's disappointment was palpable. Noah waved her forward, indicating she should precede him out of the director's office. He wanted to roar in frustration. He had learned patience during his tenure at the FBI, but had a burning desire to slay all of Abby's dragons and help her get her life back.

He was also dealing with his attraction to her, and he was beginning to have doubts about the wisdom of that. He'd kissed her, but maybe it was time to take a step back. Being in New York had reminded him of his previous life, and the agony he'd lived through as Sonya lay dying in a hospital bed while he stood by, unable to do a thing to help as the insidious cancer ravaged her body.

He didn't think he could go through that again. Loving a woman so much his heart ached, then watching her slowly fade away.

"Abby, it's been a long day. Why don't we grab a bite to eat, find a hotel and get some rest before we connect with Joe?"

She surprised him when she pivoted sharply and faced him, her mouth a grim line. "I'm not tired. Well, maybe a little, but I want answers. I'll work all night if Joe's willing."

Joe would be willing. He practically lived in his office.

Worry and trepidation shone out of her eyes. As much as he wanted to order her to eat and get a good night's sleep, he couldn't find it in his heart to do so.

"If you're sure."

She nodded and he turned toward the elevator. "Come on, then, but prepare yourself. Joe Fisher has his own little hovel that the FBI rented especially for him in the bowels of the building. As a general rule, he doesn't like people—and has very few social skills—hence his private space, but he's the best in the business."

As the elevator descended, Noah tried to erase his last images of Sonya, the day of her death. He thought he'd properly mourned her passing, but with the move to Blessing, and raising his son, Noah now wondered if that was true.

Bates whined during the elevator ride, interrupting his morbid thoughts. Abby placed a calming hand on the dog's head until they stepped off into an underground level of the building. A musty odor assailed his senses as Abby followed him down a plain, narrow hall lit by harsh, florescent lights, a few of which blinked in an annoying fashion.

They stopped in front of a door with peeling paint and Noah knocked twice. No one answered so he called through the door. "Joe, it's Noah. Open the door or I'll break it down."

A gruff voice answered back. "Hold your cotton-pickin' taters."

Abby chuckled. "I take it he's from the South?"

Noah grinned. "You two should get along great."

She poked him in the arm. "You're from Texas."

"True, but I worked in New York long enough to lose some of my roots."

She gave him a saucy grin. "Don't worry, you'll be back to normal before you know it."

The door swung open and a familiar, man of indeterminate age dressed in wrinkled khakis and a rumpled shirt stood in front of them. His hair was mussed and a pair of wire-rimmed glasses were perched on the end of his nose.

"What?"

Noah pushed his way through the door and Abby followed him. The room was a disaster. Papers littered the floor around a wastebasket and old fast-food wrappers and containers were strewed everywhere. The only saving grace was one corner of the room. It had a comfortable-looking couch, two chairs and proper lighting. Noah knew it to be his work area.

"What? No 'hello'? 'How are you, Noah? Glad to see you again'?"

Joe grumped. "I'd have called if I wanted to talk."

Noah motioned Abby forward. "This is Abby Mayfield. We need three sketches done. Already approved by Henry."

Abby held out her hand. "Nice to meet you, Joe."

The man grinned and Noah decided it'd been a while since Joe had been to the dentist for a cleaning. Joe scrutinized Abby. "You from the South?"

"Yes."

"What part?"

"Mocksville, North Carolina."

"Good. Okay, then, let's get started."

Noah shot her a befuddled look. "What is it with you

guys? Is there some sort of secret handshake between Southerners?"

Abby grinned and took a seat on the sofa. "If I told you, it wouldn't be a secret, now, would it?"

Joe snorted and Noah made himself comfortable in one of the two chairs. Joe pulled the third chair close to Abby and, with a sketch pad in hand, started firing questions.

They began with Joanne Ferguson. Joe had a litany of queries.

"Wide or narrow nose? Broad, slanted or flat forehead? Eyebrows thick or thin, slanted or straight across? Mouth—large or small? Lips—full or slim? Chin—square and strong or weak? Length, texture and thickness of hair? Hair color? Eye color?"

The list went on forever and Abby started squirming in her seat. Finally, Joe flipped the sketch pad around and Noah heard her gasp.

"It's her! It's Joanne Ferguson. Joe, you're a genius."

Joe preened and Noah grimaced. "Don't give him a big head. He knows he's good."

Sitting up straight in her chair, Abby turned to Noah with renewed energy. "But, Noah, now we have a picture of her. Can't the FBI run her through the system and find out who she is?"

Being a sharp lady, Abby didn't miss the subtle message Noah sent Joe.

"Listen, you two, I'm not some wilting Southern flower who has to have a man's protection. I have Bates, a gun and a brain. I know how to use all three. Just because I'm a choir director doesn't mean I can't protect myself."

"Steel magnolia with a thin veneer of Southern genteel," Noah muttered to Joe.

"Understood. I'm well acquainted with the type. You've never met my mother."

Abby looked like she wanted to pull her hair out, or maybe his, Noah thought, grimacing.

"What, exactly, aren't y'all telling me?"

Joe leaned back in his chair, crossed his arms over his waist and left the explanations to Noah.

Noah sighed. "It's not that simple. Yes, we'll run the picture through the FBI database and hope for the best, but that doesn't mean we'll find a match. If Ferguson and Fleming are as savvy as I think they are, they likely altered their appearances so they couldn't be identified."

Curiosity lit her eyes. "You mean like plastic surgery?"

Joe jumped in. "That's a possibility, but you can use commercial makeup and prosthetics to change your appearance. For example, you can pad your chin or nose, or change the structure of your face with an elaborate mask. And hair color can easily be changed."

Abby huffed. "The one thing I do know is Joanne Ferguson is a true brunette. I can spot a dye job a mile away. The woman sang in my choir for four months and I never saw discolored roots."

"Listen, Abby, Simon is the best. If there's not an immediate match, we now have computer programs that can add and delete facial changes and come up with possible matches. It's a long shot, but possible."

She took a deep breath. "Fine. Let's get the other two done and we'll go from there." At about four o'clock in the morning, Joe finished the last sketch.

They had a perfect rendering of Walter Fleming, at least how he appeared now, and Joe had finished the image of the unknown man who'd helped save Abby's and Noah's lives. Joe sat, studying it for a moment. He looked at Abby, then back at the sketch again, a weird look on his face.

"Well, what does he look like?" Her words came out sounding tired and cranky. Noah was feeling those sentiments himself. It had been a long day.

Joe shot Noah one of those secret FBI looks and Abby exploded, "Just show me the picture!"

Wrinkles marred Joe's forehead as he slowly turned the sketch pad around. "In answer to your question, he's a male version of you."

As soon as she caught sight of the drawing, Abby swayed. Noah was at her side in an instant, yelling for Joe to get a glass of water.

Abby ignored Noah's concern and grabbed the sketch pad Joe had thrown in his chair after running to get her some water. "Why didn't I see it sooner? I should have known. I have a brother."

Noah could only imagine what she was feeling. He took the sketch pad from her hands and placed it on the sofa cushion. "Abby, we don't know that for sure. Remember what Joe said about changing one's appearance. Whoever's after you could have planned this to throw you off their scent. In the FBI we call it misdirection."

Her eyes softened at his attempt to console her, but he pulled back, both physically and emotionally. He wasn't ready for this. Her eyes reflected a moment of hurt, but she took a deep breath and said, "Thanks, Noah. I'm okay. Maybe I'm not so tough, after all. It would never occur to me that someone would go to such lengths to hurt another human being." She paused and pressed a hand against her heart. "Do you think this is a horrible, mean trick, or is there a real possibility I may have a brother out there somewhere?"

"Anything is possible, Abby, but there is one thing

I know. I'll do everything in my power to find out the truth. Why don't we grab a bite to eat and get some sleep?"

Joe came rushing into the room with a glass of water in hand. The poor guy looked terrified of a crying woman. Noah had been known to have the same weakness.

Abby stood and gave Joe a big hug, and Noah's gut clenched when her arms went around his old friend. "Thanks for everything, Joe." She brushed a friendly kiss against his cheek and a light blush covered his face. "We'll come and visit when this is over."

"Y'all do that now, and let me know what happens."

"We will," Abby said, and Noah led the way out the door.

The next morning, Noah awoke and stretched the kinks and soreness out of his body before swinging his legs over the side of the bed. Between the car crash and the explosion at Abby's grandmother's house, he had more than a few aches and pains.

The clock on the nightstand read seven thirty. It was much later than he usually slept, but they hadn't gotten to bed until after five o'clock in the morning. They could have gone to bed sooner, but Abby refused to stay in the condo the FBI kept on hand for various uses. She claimed it wasn't proper for them to stay in the same space, so he'd had to hunt down a hotel that allowed dogs and had two rooms available in Manhattan during the wee hours of the morning. It aggravated him, but he also respected her for sticking to her principles.

In his line of work, he didn't come across women like Abby Mayfield often. She was beautiful, with her soft blond hair, petite stature and big brown eyes. But it was her quirky, strong, interesting personality that drew him in like a magnet. A magnet he was working hard to disengage from.

He grabbed his cell phone, disconnected it from the charger and called Abby in the room next door.

"Noah?" she whispered.

"It's time to rise and shine."

"Noah," she said, louder this time. "Someone's rattling the doorknob to my room. It sounds like they're trying to jimmy the lock."

"Hold tight," he shouted into the phone before throwing the device onto the bed. A surge of adrenaline shot through him, alleviating all signs of morning drowsiness as he ran for his door. Flinging it open, he spotted the back of a man disappearing through the stairwell door. Abby's door creaked open and he yelled over his shoulder, "Get back inside and lock the door. Stay put until I return."

He heard the door slam shut. Knowing she was safe, he lit out after the man, but by the time he reached the ground floor, the guy had disappeared. Noah bent over and placed his hands on his knees, trying to catch his breath. His mind raced with possibilities. From his brief glance at the man, he couldn't tell if it was Walter Fleming.

He slapped his thighs in frustration. Who wanted Abby dead, and more important, why? Nothing made sense. He turned back toward the stairs, and determination and fear for Abby's life hurried his climb up the steps. He took a deep breath and centered himself while approaching her door. He knocked and she threw it wide-open, flying into his arms.

He pulled her arms from around his neck and took

a step back. Abby moved away, a confused and embarrassed look on her face.

"Oh, I'm sorry. I thought after that kiss…"

Noah held out a hand in supplication. "Abby…"

She backed away farther. "No problem, I completely understand. Now, did you get a good look at the guy? Did he have a gun?"

Noah wanted to say more, to explain, but maybe it was better this way.

"I'm fine. He got away. I couldn't identify the man."

She gave a jerky nod. "Okay, then. As long as you're safe."

Noah ached to comfort her and remove her fear, but gave a brisk nod instead. "Let's get dressed, grab some breakfast here in the hotel and head back to the FBI office."

Abby pulled her pink robe tightly around her waist. "Yes, okay. I'll be ready in half an hour."

Noah left her room and returned to his own. He closed off his emotions and concentrated on the investigation—what steps they should take next—while showering and dressing for the day. He buried the image of Abby's soft brown eyes widened in fear. He would never have allowed her to stay in a room alone if Bates hadn't been with her. That dog was the only reason he'd gotten any sleep at all.

FIFTEEN

Entering the FBI building, Abby felt a measure of relief and safety. She hadn't realized how tense she'd been until this very moment. She thanked God her grandmother had insisted she buy a protection dog before moving to Texas. Noah was noted in his profession as being the best, but he was only one man.

She squelched her emotions concerning Noah. One minute he was kissing her, and the next minute he was pulling away. His actions had hurt, but she had enough on her plate without worrying about his mixed signals.

She followed him through the hustle and bustle of the FBI room toward the big office at the back. A few greetings were yelled across the room, but he barely acknowledged them. He'd been all business since leaving the hotel. Not that they had a relationship or anything—he'd only kissed her once but, still, they'd been through a lot together.

She wasn't even sure she wanted a close bond with a man in such a dangerous profession. She sighed as she followed him into his former boss's office with Bates trotting at her side. Life used to be a lot simpler. And she thought dealing with church politics was complicated.

It was nothing compared to what Noah did every day, putting his life at risk when he went to work.

He had called ahead. Everyone was waiting, crammed into the office. Greetings were short and they got down to business after everyone took a seat.

Noah fired the opening salvo. "Someone tried to break into Abby's hotel room early this morning. I chased them down the stairwell, but lost them. I can't identify the man. As far as I could tell, he doesn't resemble anyone we've dealt with so far. The security cameras were useless—bad lighting in the stairwell and the guy wore a baseball cap. He was smart enough to keep his face turned away from the cameras."

It was depressing how few clues they had, Abby mused.

The door banged open and Simon came rushing in, clutching a file folder in his hand. His rumpled clothes looked suspiciously similar to the ones he had worn the previous day. Abby wondered if any of the FBI agents ever slept as all eyes focused on Simon.

He slouched into the empty chair beside Abby. "Sorry. I was up late studying for an exam."

Abby remembered Noah had said Simon was also attending school. "You have an awful lot on your plate," she whispered.

Simon studied the toe of his scuffed sneaker. "It was this or go to jail."

His annoyed tone tickled Abby. "Good choice."

"Yeah," he said before Director Wilson took firm control of the meeting.

"Simon, what do you have for us?"

Simon straightened in his chair, and Abby thought having him work for the FBI while in college was a good idea. He was experiencing things most young men his age would never see in a lifetime.

"I'm still eliminating license plates that begin with the letters *C-A-M*, specifically searching for a cream or beige sedan. Franny's running Joe's sketches of Joanne Ferguson, Walter Fleming and the unknown guy as we speak. I'll let you know if anything pops."

Abby remembered Franny as the name of Simon's computer and smiled. It was good to forget about Noah's cold shoulder for a while.

"I've been trying to track down information on Abby's parents' backgrounds, but their lives are a total blank until right before she was born in North Carolina. Their Social Security numbers are bogus."

Abby stiffened. Noah had asked Simon to search her parents' backgrounds without talking to her first? That was the reason for going to her grandmother's house in the first place, but how dare he do so without her permission? One of her biggest fears was that they'd find something that would hurt Grammy. Surely they could figure out who was after her without destroying the only family she had left. Noah must have found their Social Security numbers mixed in with the box of pictures they'd saved. She shot Noah a disgruntled look, but he still had that stony-face thing going.

Director Wilson addressed the group. "We need to look at Abby's parents' and husband's deaths."

Nausea churned in her stomach, but she swallowed hard and gritted her teeth. She would get through this. Noah hadn't even glanced at her at the announcement, and it hurt, but she held her head high and addressed the group.

"As I've explained to Noah, my husband died three

years ago in a car crash. There were no other vehicles involved. The police reported it as a terrible accident."

Memories swamped her, the loss of a husband and an unborn child so close together, but she pushed them away. "My parents died in a car crash while vacationing in Jackson Hole, Wyoming. It, too, was deemed an accident. There were no other vehicles involved that time, either."

Describing both accidents at the same time did sound suspicious.

"Why did they choose Jackson Hole for a vacation?" the director asked.

The question threw her off balance. "I don't know. I was only six at the time. They left me with Grammy. She might have some information that will help."

"I understand your grandmother is in a hospital in North Carolina in an induced coma. Is that right?" Director Wilson asked.

"Yes, she is, because whoever these people are, they attacked her and put her there." Abby didn't even try to hide the vehemence in her voice. Every time she thought of her grandmother lying in that sterile hospital bed, it broke her heart.

Alex Ridenhour spoke for the first time that morning. "My team will comb through the reports on her parents' and husband's deaths. We'll also see what we can find out about their trip to Jackson Hole, but it's going to be a cold trail."

A million thoughts swamped Abby's tired, overwhelmed mind, but something kept nagging her. She couldn't quite put her finger on it...then suddenly it became crystal clear.

"Y'all can do whatever you want to, but I'm going to Wyoming."

The room burst into chaotic speech.

"You're a civilian. I won't be held responsible for placing you at risk." This from Noah's former boss, Henry Wilson.

"No way! You shouldn't even be allowed to accompany Noah," Alex Ridenhour added his two cents' worth.

"Absolutely not. I forbid it." The last, and most hurtful, objection came from Noah.

Bates released a low growl and Abby placed a calming hand on his head. He had taken a position on the floor beside her. "That's right, I'm a civilian. Y'all can't tell me where I can go or what I can do. I'll accompany Noah anywhere he goes, and if he doesn't want me tagging along, I'll go by myself. As a teacher, I know how to get people to open up and talk. I expect I'll find out more than any of you. I have Bates and my grandmother's Glock. I can take care of myself."

Noah's glacial mask had fallen away, replaced by a look of horror. Good! She was sick and tired of his stony, closed expression.

"Why, Abby?"

Her anger subsided. She knew he was worried about her, and she appreciated that, but she would stand firm. "I think there are secrets in Jackson Hole. I intend to unearth every one of them. I will not risk my grandmother getting hurt again." She took a deep breath. "And if that means rooting out every dark, nasty family secret, I will."

She realized, in that moment, in order to stop these terrible people, she and Grammy both would have to deal with whatever secrets they uncovered. It was the only way to stay safe and be able to move forward with their lives.

After shedding her reluctance at delving into family

secrets, Abby felt free and wanted to get on with it. She stood and looked straight at Noah. "Well, are you coming or not?"

He stood, but talked to the guys before following her out of the room.

"Alex, I'll call if we run into trouble."

"No problem."

"Simon, let me know as soon as you find anything."

"You got it," came his reply.

Abby could only imagine the looks of pity Noah received from his former colleagues, but now that she had decided to open her family's can of worms, she had a burning desire to know the truth. Good or bad.

"Lord, help me," she said softly under her breath, as Noah followed her out the door and through the maze of cubicles.

Noah stole a glance at Abby as she stared out of the plane window while they waited for takeoff. He knew he'd hurt her, but it was for the best, even though it left an empty, hollow place deep inside him.

After leaving the FBI offices, they had gathered their luggage, checked out of the hotel, grabbed a bite to eat and made reservations to fly to Jackson Hole. The last-minute tickets cost a mint, but Noah refused to allow Abby to pay the airfare, even though she tried to insist.

He paid extra for bulkhead seats so Bates would have plenty of room to lie at their feet. Abby had attired the dog with his special vest, but she allowed several kids to pet him as they boarded the plane.

Even though Noah had stepped back from their budding relationship, he wanted and needed to understand exactly what had happened to her husband and parents. In his line of work, he'd seen the most congenial of people turn out to be serial killers.

He stayed quiet while she sent several texts.

"Everything okay?"

She tucked her phone inside her purse. "Yes. I had to check on several of my students. If you'll remember, we have a big recital coming up, along with the Christmas play. That's if we can find a place to have them, since the church is gone."

Her voice wobbled at the end of her sentence and it shattered the thin layer of ice he'd been building around his heart.

They were given instructions to buckle up, and he waited until the plane was fully in the air before shifting sideways in his seat. "Abby, listen to me. The explosion at the church wasn't your fault. We'll track down the culprits and they'll spend the rest of their lives in prison."

"That won't pay for the church," she grumbled, and Noah was glad to see her spirits lift.

"I'm sure the church has insurance."

She turned in her seat and fire lit her eyes. Good. He'd take irritation any day over despondency.

"I wish I'd kept more of the life insurance money. I'd rebuild the church myself. You know how those insurance companies are. They never pay enough to restore things like they were."

"If the money comes up short, I have no doubt you can raise what's needed. There are a lot of good people in Blessing who will contribute to seeing their church rebuilt, and they won't blame you. From what I've heard, the people of Blessing love their new choir director."

She squirmed in her seat, as if embarrassed. "Well, I love them, too, but you're not going to sweeten me up with pretty words. I'm still upset that you asked Alex to look into the deaths of my husband and parents without talking to me first. Not that I don't think it's a good idea, I want these people caught and I'm willing to lay my life open to make it happen. I just wish you'd had the courtesy to speak to me before you brought it up in front of everyone."

He cleared his throat. "Abby, I'll do whatever it takes to keep you safe, and if that means upsetting you with my methods, then so be it."

"Listen, Noah, I know you mean well, and I appreciate all your help, but I'm at the center of this mess. I don't know what's going on, but I mean to find out. If that means dragging my family's name through the mud, then I'm willing to do that. My grandmother's life is more important than anything."

"Your life is more important than anything, too."

"Well, we should make plans for when we reach Jackson Hole. Like where we should start first."

Noah straightened in his seat and faced forward. "I called the sheriff in Jackson while we were waiting in the airport. We'll rent a car when we land and head straight to his office. He's expecting us. Why don't you close your eyes and get some rest?"

Noah followed his own advice, hoping Abby would do the same, but his mind raced with the information they had and didn't have. Why did Abby's parents decide to take that fateful trip to Jackson Hole, and why did the pictures of an unknown child in their arms keep popping up? Noah was afraid Abby wouldn't be happy with the answers.

SIXTEEN

Abby woke up with a start when the plane's wheels bumped against the landing strip. She checked on Bates. He had been trained to fly, but wasn't happy about it. His ears stood up straight, but he didn't whine. Abby patted his head. "Good boy," she crooned.

Beside her, Noah chuckled. "I've never been thrilled about flying, either."

Abby yawned. "I never would have thought I could sleep after everything that's happened."

Noah stretched his legs out. "I had a few winks myself."

He shifted in his seat and Abby glanced at him. "Is something wrong?"

His eyes bored into hers, as if seeking answers. "Abby, are you sure you're ready to deal with what we might find? The place where your parents died?"

Was she ready? "To be honest, I don't know, but I'm going to dig as hard as I can and ask God for His grace and protection no matter what we discover."

He studied her a moment longer and gave a short nod. "Okay."

The plane landed and people were lined up in the aisle trying to be the first off. They waited until the last person passed by, then Noah grabbed their carry-on luggage from the overhead bin.

Abby bid the flight attendants goodbye.

Stepping off the small airplane, she took a deep breath of frigid air and smiled for the first time in what seemed like centuries. It was November, and snow covered everything. It looked like a winter wonderland.

Noah grinned. "Beautiful, isn't it?"

"Yes," she breathed. Fog puffed out of her mouth. She pulled her coat tighter around her. "And cold. You've been here before?"

He had both their bags and carried them as if they weighed ounces instead of pounds. "Yep. Couple of years back I came to Jackson on business."

Abby assumed that meant FBI business, but she didn't want to discuss investigations. For just a few minutes, as they walked toward the airport building, she wanted to immerse herself in God's glorious creations. Pine tree boughs hung low due to the weight of the snow, and red cardinals stood out in stark relief. A few flakes swirled around her, and Abby thought Jackson Hole a romantic place. A gush of warm air hit her when they stepped inside the terminal. After retrieving their checked luggage and weapons, they rented a SUV and were on their way.

She continued her moments of peace by staring out the window, when all of a sudden, she saw a huge mountain to their left with skiers racing down the steep slope. "Wow. That's gorgeous."

"Jackson Hole consists of two parts. We're in the town of Jackson, and that mountain you're admiring is Jackson's ski mountain. A few miles to the west is a place called Teton Village. The Teton mountain is the steepest ski slope in the United States. Jackson Hole is also one of the coldest. A bus runs between Jackson and Teton Village every thirty minutes all day, every day, carrying tourists between the two places."

Noah pulled the SUV to the curb in front of the police station and Abby's momentary peace was shattered. She didn't want to deal with the ugly things going on in her life, but she didn't have a choice. She grabbed the door handle and slid out of the car before Noah had a chance to do the gentlemanly thing and help her out. It was better if he didn't touch her, considering the recent past. She was dying to know what had caused him to back off, but now wasn't the time to delve into things probably better left alone.

She wanted answers and she wanted her life back. The only way to make that happen was to face her problems head-on. Grammy would be proud. As if sensing her resolve, Noah moved in front of her and opened the station door. The heat warmed her body, but she was still chilled at the thought of what was to come.

The woman at the front desk called out, "Can I help you?"

Abby felt more comfortable here than at the FBI office. Just like her, these were small-town people. A Christmas tree with children's names hanging in place of ornaments stood lit in one corner. The front desk had been decorated with a strand of greenery.

Noah took the lead. "Sheriff Hoyt is expecting us. Noah Galloway and Abigail Mayfield."

The older woman carried a few extra pounds and was bundled in a heavy Christmas sweater and slacks. Her eyes crinkled merrily when she spoke. She reminded Abby of a sweet little grandmother.

"Ethan told me you were coming. Y'all are a long way from home." Abby knew the woman was dying to know what they were doing in Jackson Hole. She considered it a credit to Sheriff Hoyt that he hadn't spread their business around the office. Noah took care of the woman's nosiness by raising a brow.

She straightened an already neat stack of papers on her desk. "Yes, well, his office is down the hall, first door on the left."

"Thank you," Noah said, and headed in that direction, but Abby lingered behind. She had a few seeds to sow. Abby read the name tag on the desk—Mrs. Wanda Armstrong—and figured the woman probably knew everything that happened in the town of Jackson, and she was about the right age. Wanda would have been a young woman when Abby's parents came to Jackson all those years ago.

"Mrs. Armstrong—"

"Call me Wanda."

It was a good start. "And please call me Abby."

Wanda stuck out a hand. "Nice to meetcha, Abby."

Abby shook her hand, propped her elbows on the raised front part of the desk and leaned forward, inviting a good gossip. "Sorry about Noah. You know how men are, worried to death somebody will impede their investigations."

Wanda bobbed her head. "I know what you mean. Sometimes it's the small, overlooked details that solve a problem."

Bingo! Abby had her. Noah and Sheriff Hoyt could conduct their investigation the way they saw fit, but Abby would stir the local gossip pot and hopefully come up with some information.

Abby lowered her voice. "We're here because twenty-two years ago, my parents died in a car crash in Jackson."

Wanda commiserated. "Oh, I'm sorry to hear that. What were their names?"

"Mary and Lee Beauchamp. My last name is Mayfield. I married, but my husband was also the victim of a car crash. My maiden name is Beauchamp."

Wanda clucked. "You poor dear. To lose one's parents and husband, too. Is that why you're in Jackson? To find out more about your parents' deaths?"

Abby didn't want her life story bandied all over town, so she skirted around the truth. "Partly. Some new information has come to light and Sheriff Galloway has reason to believe that their deaths might not have been an accident."

Wanda's hand flew to her heart. "Oh, my."

Abby grabbed a pen and piece of paper sitting on top of the desk and scribbled down her cell number. She passed it to Wanda. "If you know of anyone who might remember my parents being here all those years ago, I sure would appreciate it."

Wanda grabbed the paper, determination lighting her eyes. "I'll start calling around now."

Abby stood straight. Her work here was done. "Thank you so much. I sure do appreciate people like you, kind enough to help a stranger in need."

It was the right thing to say. She hurried down the hall and heard a heavy tread coming toward her. She met Noah halfway.

"What were you doing?" he asked.

She gave him a smug smile. "Just planting a few seeds, Noah, just planting a few seeds."

Noah let it go. He'd been surprised before entering Sheriff Hoyt's office to realize Abby wasn't behind him.

She had something up her sleeve, but he'd find out later what she was up to.

Sheriff Hoyt rose from his desk after they knocked and he invited them in.

Hoyt was tall, about six-four, with the weathered face of a rancher. He didn't wear a standard uniform, but was decked out in faded jeans and a Western shirt. From his last visit, several years back, Noah remembered that Hoyt, along with being the town's sheriff, also owned a spread a few miles outside of town. He ran a small herd of cattle, if memory served.

"Noah, good to see you again." He turned to Abby. "And who's this pretty little lady with you?"

Noah also remembered that Hoyt was single, his wife having passed on from a heart attack early in their marriage. Ethan Hoyt was about Noah's age, and jealousy shot straight through Noah, causing his reply to come out short and brisk, even though it was his choice not to pursue Abby. "This is Abigail Mayfield. Abby, meet Ethan Hoyt, sheriff of Jackson."

Hoyt's eyebrows rose at the shortness of Noah's tone, and curiosity crossed his features as he studied Noah and Abby. He held out a hand to Abby. "Nice to meet you, Abigail Mayfield. Everyone take a seat and we'll see how I can help you. Noah didn't tell me your reason for visiting our fair city."

Noah didn't pull any punches. "Someone is trying to kill Abby and we have very few leads." The affable, small-town sheriff disappeared and Hoyt's eyes sharpened. Noah had researched Hoyt the last time he'd dealt with him. The good sheriff had left a job in Chicago as a top detective for a simpler, safer life in Wyoming after he married. He'd decided to stay on after his wife died.

"Tell me more."

It took a while for Noah to fill Hoyt in on everything that had happened in North Carolina and Texas. He added everything the FBI was tracking down. "I'll have Joe send copies of the sketches of Ferguson, Fleming and the unknown man to your office."

Hoyt whistled long and hard. "And you think Abby's parents' deaths are connected?"

Noah leaned back in his chair. "That's what we're here to find out."

Hoyt nodded at Bates and addressed Abby. "Is that a trained protection dog?"

"Yes, but he's also a pet," Abby said. Noah choked back a chuckle. He couldn't wait to see Hoyt's face when Abby used one of her commands.

Hoyt's chair creaked when he followed Noah's lead and leaned back. "My resources are at your disposal. I'll help any way I can. If you run into trouble, call me immediately."

"First, we'll need the accident reports. Alex is going to follow up on that, but I'd like to take a look at them."

Hoyt grimaced and Noah's heart sank.

"We had a fire several years ago. The town had just hired someone to computerize all the records, but they went up in flames. It should have been done years ago, but the county budget is always tight."

Noah sat there, thinking. "Was it arson?"

"It was, but we never caught the arsonist." Hoyt looked at him sharply. "You think there's a connection?"

Noah stood. "I don't know, but it seems awfully convenient. Thanks for your help. I'll be in touch."

Hoyt touched the brim of an imaginary hat. "Ma'am. And I'll be waiting to hear from you, Galloway. Keep me posted."

Noah followed Abby out of the office, his mind racing a mile a minute. Had the fire been set to destroy a specific accident report, or was it coincidental?

Abby pulled away and moved to the front desk when the woman with the big hair they'd met earlier waved her down. Noah followed and was jerked out of his musings when he caught the last part of the conversation.

"What did you say?" he bluntly asked the woman. The name plate on the desk said Wanda Armstrong. "Wanda," he added for good measure.

Wanda gave him a wide smile. "I was just telling Abby that I tracked down where her parents stayed when they visited Jackson all those years ago. It's a bed-and-breakfast just down the street. Old Mrs. Denton has owned the place forever, and she fondly remembers Mary and Lee Beauchamp staying there, but that's not the best part. Mrs. Denton said the nice couple also had the cutest little boy with them."

The information hit Noah like a steam engine but he knew it had to be worse for Abby. The unidentified child in the pictures? Could it be?

One look at Abby's face had Noah thanking Wanda for the information and pulling Abby out the door. She was shell-shocked and her hands were freezing. He herded Bates into the back seat and prodded Abby into the passenger seat. He turned the ignition on and put the heat on full blast. Her expression reminded him of soldiers coming back from war. The empty, dazed looks in their eyes. It scared him spitless.

"Abby. Look at me."

No response. Noah grabbed both her hands and blew on them. "Abby. Please say something. I need you here with me."

Finally, finally, she turned her head toward him. "The child in the picture…"

"I know. We'll find out what's going on. I promise."

She closed her eyes, as if in prayer, and Noah said a silent one himself. He begged God to help them solve this case before someone else got hurt or, worse, killed. The people after Abby meant business and he was the only one standing between them and her.

Bates whined and shook Abby out of her frozen state. "I'm fine. I'll be okay in just a minute."

She took a deep breath and straightened her shoulders. "It's just that… It was big shock, knowing my parents came to Jackson with a child."

"I know, but, Abby… Look at me." She cut her eyes toward him and relief hit him square in the gut. "I promise we'll find out what's going on and I'll be with you every step of the way."

She nodded briskly and he missed the sweet smiles she used to throw his way, before he decided to protect his heart from any unforeseeable sorrow.

"Thank you, Noah. You've gone well beyond the call of duty."

Duty wasn't what was prodding him to stay at Abby's side. He ignored that thought and concentrated on the present.

"Can you handle staying at the bed-and-breakfast where your parents stayed so we can scope out the place and talk to Mrs. Denton?"

She jerked her chin up and down. "I am definitely ready to stay at Mrs. Denton's. The sooner we find answers, the sooner we can go home."

Noah buried his desire to wrap his arms around her and protect her from this nightmare. They had to move forward. He put the car in Drive and headed toward the bed-and-breakfast. Within ten minutes, he parked in front of a quaint inn. He grabbed their bags while Abby released Bates from the back seat and attached his leash. They mounted the steps that led to a beautiful wraparound porch.

Abby grabbed the front doorknob. "Wanda said she'd call ahead and let Mrs. Denton know we were coming. Maybe she'll have something we can eat."

Noah felt like a heel. With so much happening, he hadn't even thought about food since lunch. Then the fine hair on his neck pricked, and Bates released a low growl just as Abby swung the door open.

Before he could grab her elbow, removing her from potential harm, she took a step inside and started screaming.

SEVENTEEN

Abby was in shock after she stepped into the bed-and-breakfast and spotted an older woman crumpled on the floor. A small puddle of blood had gathered beneath her head and more was streaming out.

It took a few seconds for her to realize someone had grasped her shoulders and was shaking her. "Noah?"

"I'm here. Abby, you have to stay calm and help me. Call 911. I'll check on the woman."

She took a deep breath and did her best to get control. But after everything that had happened over the last few weeks, she was using her last reserves. "Is it Mrs. Denton?" she whispered.

"Call 911. Tell them to contact Sheriff Hoyt."

No! It couldn't be. "Noah, do you think this has something to do with me?"

His voice firmed and it acted as a catalyst, prodding Abby into action. "Call 911. Now."

Fumbling inside her purse, she dug out her cell phone and punched in the numbers.

"Nine-one-one. How can I help you?"

Abby's words came out in a nervous stream. "We're at Mrs. Denton's bed-and-breakfast. I don't know the name of the establishment, but you have to hurry. We just arrived and there's a lady on the floor with blood seeping from the back of her head. And please notify Sheriff Hoyt."

"Stay on the phone, ma'am. I'm dispatching an ambulance and notifying the closest patrol car. They'll arrive on scene in less than five minutes."

"Thank you," Abby whispered. If Mrs. Denton had been hurt because of her, she didn't know what she'd do. Maybe it would be better to let Noah handle things. Maybe she should go back to North Carolina and stay by Grammy's side.

Abby held the cell phone in a death grip and closed her eyes. *Dear Lord, please show me what to do. I don't want anyone else hurt because of me.* A peace that could only come from above settled on her like gossamer wings, giving comfort and the sure knowledge that she was to see this through, no matter the cost. *Okay, Lord.*

"Abby, she's alive. Open the front door but stay in the house, and guide the ambulance attendants inside as soon as they arrive."

She breathed a short prayer of thanks that the woman lived. The ambulance arrived first, careening down the road and screeching to a halt in the middle of the street. Abby waved both hands above her head and yelled when they piled out of the vehicle. "Here! Over here!"

A man and a woman carrying medical bags ran up the sidewalk and Abby motioned them inside the house. She followed, but stayed out of the way.

"It's old Mrs. Denton, alright," one of them said.

Sheriff Hoyt walked through the door and stood beside Abby. They stayed quiet while the EMTs checked out Mrs. Denton.

While they were doing their business, the older woman regained consciousness and slapped their hands away. "I'm fine. Just let me get my bearings," she groused.

Abby took her first normal breath since arriving at the bed-and-breakfast. *Thank You, Lord.*

Determined to get on her feet, Mrs. Denton allowed the attendants to help her rise and they guided her to a chair. They were checking the back of her head when she happened to look up. She reminded Abby of a sweet little grandma until she opened her mouth.

"Who are you?" she sniped at Noah. She cut her eyes toward the sheriff. "I know who you are."

Abby walked forward and knelt in front of her, taking a cold, blue-veined hand in hers. "I'm Abby Mayfield and this is Noah Galloway. Wanda was supposed to call and let you know we were coming."

Mrs. Denton grinned. "She did. You're a pretty little thing."

Sheriff Hoyt broke up the conversation. "Mrs. Denton, did you get a look at the intruders?"

A canny gaze swung back to the sheriff. "I would have if they hadn't had their heads covered with ski masks. Half the people who come in here are wearing those things after skiing. I didn't think a thing about it when they walked through the door."

Both attendants stood up. "We'll take her to the hospital, do a few X-rays, but from what I can see, it's not a deep wound. She needs to be checked for a concussion."

Abby hid a grin as Mrs. Denton faced off with the ambulance attendants. The older woman reminded her of Grammy. "I'm not going to the hospital. That place is for sick people. I just hit my head on the corner of the check-in desk when one of those hoodlums shoved me."

Sheriff Hoyt nodded his head toward the door and the attendants backed off after dressing the wound.

"Call the hospital if you need us, and wake her several times throughout the night to make sure she's okay," the woman said, and they scurried out the door.

Bright, intelligent eyes shone out from a roadmap of wrinkles when Mrs. Denton zeroed in on Abby. "You look just like your mama."

Abby's heart took a giant leap in her chest and she knelt back down in front of the older lady. "What do you know of my mama?"

"Wanda called and told me what was going on. I remember everything about that lovely couple—the Beauchamps—and that cute little boy." She got a faraway look in her eyes. "They only stayed at my place that one time. I always kenned the old sheriff was wrong. That car accident weren't no accident."

Please, dear Lord, give us some answers. Abby picked up the woman's hand again. "Anything you can remember about that time will help."

The woman's eyes cleared and focused on Abby. "That's what those men wanted, you know, the ones who pushed me. They told me to keep my mouth shut about the Beauchamps or they'd come back and finish the job. One of 'em wanted to kill me, but the other one said it would cause too much trouble for them, seeing as how the FBI was already on their tail."

Mrs. Denton peered up at Noah. "You FBI, boy?"

"Used to be, ma'am. I'm a sheriff in Blessing, Texas, now."

She cackled and looked back at Abby. "Boy's got manners. I like him."

Sheriff Hoyt had stayed silent and Abby was grateful. She wanted answers. "Did they say anything else, the men who attacked you?"

"Nope, just told me to keep my mouth shut."

Abby didn't want anything to happen to the dear old lady. "Maybe it's best if you do keep quiet."

Noah shifted on his feet, but Sheriff Hoyt stayed silent.

Mrs. Denton cackled. "Darlin', I done lived long enough for two people. You don't have to worry about me. Only God knows when my time is up."

The older woman licked her lips and Abby turned toward Noah. "Get Mrs. Denton a glass of water, please."

Within a couple of minutes, he presented Mrs. Denton with a full glass. She drank half of it and Abby removed it from her hand.

"Anyways, it was a long time ago now, when your mama and daddy visited my establishment. Can't remember exactly how many years, but it was two weeks before Christmas. What's interesting is, after they got here, a woman brought a boy to them. He was maybe about ten years old or so."

Her eyes filled with sorrow and Abby's stomach clenched.

Abby swallowed the lump in her throat. She had to know everything. "And what about the accident? Why didn't you agree with the old sheriff?"

"Well, the night it happened—the last night of their stay—I couldn't sleep and went down to the kitchen to heat up some milk. I heard a car start up and glanced out the window. It was the Beauchamps' car. The whole thing seemed odd to me, so I went to their room and knocked. No one answered the door and I used my master key to get inside. The room was empty."

Abby gathered her courage and asked the question burning in her gut, "And the child? Do you think he left with them?"

Mrs. Denton shook her head. "That's the thing.

That's why the old sheriff didn't put much stock in my theory that the couple was taking off with the boy. I only saw the car drive off, not who was in the car. The woman who brought him could have picked up the child when I wasn't around. The old sheriff ruled it an accident and that was that."

Abby briefly wondered why her parents hadn't brought her with them to Jackson Hole instead of leaving her at Grammy's. The whole thing was very strange.

Abby looked over her shoulder at Noah. "If the accident reports are gone, how will we know if the child was in the car?"

Mrs. Denton answered her question. "The child was nowhere to be seen at the accident site 'cause I asked the old sheriff. He claimed there were only two people in the car, identified as Mr. and Mrs. Beauchamp."

Sheriff Hoyt stepped forward. "Mrs. Denton, since you refuse to go to the hospital, you should get some rest, but you'll need to be checked on throughout the night."

Abby stood and held out a hand. "Let me help you to your bedroom."

The older woman grinned. "You're as nice as your mama."

Abby's heart felt like it was bleeding inside at the thought of her parents and the boy. Who was he? And why did someone drop off the child for them to visit with in Jackson Hole?

As they made their way upstairs, Mrs. Denton told Abby they should make themselves at home. There was food in the kitchen that could be heated, and they could pick any rooms in the place as she had an empty house at the moment.

After settling their hostess, Abby closed the bedroom

door quietly and made her way back to the kitchen. Her stomach growled when she caught the scent of fried chicken. As she entered the room, Abby saw that Bates had a dish filled with dog food on the floor and Noah had laid two filled plates on the table. They both sat down. She said grace and they ate in silence. When they finished, Noah placed the dishes in the sink.

"We'll talk tomorrow. We need sleep. I'll wake Mrs. Denton in an hour and check on her."

She agreed. Noah picked two rooms next to each other. Abby entered her room and glanced at the bathroom. She should at least brush her teeth. Instead, after slipping her gun under her pillow, she fell back onto the bed, fully dressed, and crashed.

Abby had no idea what time it was when something disturbed her sleep. She patted the bedcovers and found Bates sitting on his haunches, totally focused on the window. He released a low, intense warning growl. Her heart started beating wildly when he released a second, more lethal growl. Abby followed Bates's line of vision and saw a man with one leg thrown over the inside of the windowsill. She reached for the Glock hidden under her pillow.

"I have a gun and my dog will rip your throat out." She was proud of how strong her words sounded, but in truth, her hands were shaking.

"Please, don't shoot. I'm not here to hurt you. I'm here to help."

Abby didn't trust the soft, pleading voice. She should scream for Noah, but instinct told her to find out what this man wanted. "Help me how? Who are you?"

He slowly climbed into the room and placed both feet on the floor, but froze when Bates snarled.

"It's safer if you don't know anything about me. I'm only here to warn you. You have to go into hiding. Permanently. Don't trust anyone. The people after you, their arms reach far and wide, from local law enforcement to politicians in high positions, and they want you dead."

A chill iced her body, but Abby followed her gut. "They're after you, too, aren't they? Tell me. Maybe I can help."

Silence, then he said, "I made sure they believe I'm dead."

Noah must have heard something because a hard knock shook their connecting door.

"Abby? Are you okay? Open the door. Now!"

The man in the shadows slipped back out the open window. He grabbed a tree branch close to the opening before glancing back at her, but she couldn't make out his face.

"Don't trust him, either," he said before fleeing.

"Abby! Open the door, or I'll break it down."

Abby scooted out of bed and closed the window as the man's words pounded in her head. *Don't trust him, either.* She needed time to think and assess. Throwing on her robe, she stopped and took a deep breath before forcing a yawn and opening the door.

"Where's the fire?" She forced another yawn and wiped her face of emotion.

Noah gave her a hard stare and pushed his way into the room, flipping the light switch on as he passed. He prowled around and stuck his head inside the bathroom. He came back and faced her. "I could have sworn I heard Bates growl."

Abby waved a negligent hand in the air. "Oh, that.

Sometimes Bates hears a squirrel or something outside and takes issue with it."

His eyes glittered with mistrust. Abby hated seeing that expression return, but she needed time to think things through.

He turned toward the connecting door. "Yell if something happens. The walls are thin in this old house."

Abby closed the door behind him and leaned against it and shut her eyes. Had she just made the biggest mistake of her life in not confiding in Noah?

EIGHTEEN

Noah awoke the next morning with one thought. Abby was lying.

He had interrogated some of the most sophisticated liars in the criminal world, and he knew Abby Mayfield had lied through her teeth. But about what? And why? Even though he'd stepped back emotionally, he'd been on the verge of fully trusting her, but now she'd blown that out of the water. Was her secret something sinister? Did she know more about her husband's and parents' deaths than she'd revealed? Had someone been in her room last night? Did she sneak them in through the window?

He grabbed his cell phone off the charger on the nightstand when it buzzed. It was six o'clock and he hadn't gotten much sleep the night before.

"What?" he barked.

"And good morning to you, too, Mr. Sunshine." Alex sounded rested and ready for the day. His old partner's enthusiasm soured Noah's mood even more.

"It's early. You got something for me?"

"Is that any way to treat your old partner? Hey! Maybe I'd like to get out of the big city, too. You need a deputy in Blessing?"

Noah growled into the phone.

"Fine. I have information on the husband's death."

Noah came awake with startling clarity. "Spill."

"I sent Toby snooping."

Toby was a private investigator Alex and Noah had used on occasion when they wanted work done on the down low. In other words, they used him—someone not connected with the FBI—when they wanted to hide something from their superiors.

"Why use Toby?" Noah's gut burned. He didn't know if it was because of Abby's lies, or the fact that Alex calling in Toby meant this thing was big and went high up the food chain of law enforcement. How high was the question.

"The husband's death appears to be clean. It was ruled an accident and Simon didn't come across anything to contradict that, but here's the interesting part. Simon found a sealed file buried deep within the FBI's system on the parents' deaths."

Noah squeezed his eyes shut. Simon was supposed to be reforming, not breaking into sealed FBI files, but at this point, he didn't care. He wanted to know what Simon had found.

"And?"

"There's a police report on the parents' accident in Jackson Hole. It shouldn't even be in the FBI files if it was a mere accident. Simon decided to snoop when we found out about the suspicious fire in Jackson that destroyed all police records."

Noah loosened his hand on the cell phone and took a deep breath. "Cut to the chase, Ridenhour."

"Fine, but you sure know how to take the fun out of everything."

He hurried on before Noah had a chance to blast him.

"The report states that Lee Beauchamp lost control of his car and ran off a steep embankment. No other vehicles involved. The key here is that the accident shouldn't have been an FBI case."

Noah's gut burned with acid.

A vision of Abby and him being run off the road played in his mind.

"What about the old sheriff in Jackson? Maybe he'll have some answers. Is Toby tracking him down? I'd love to have a chat with him."

"Well, now, that's a problem. Toby did track him down. The old sheriff died two months after Abby's parents."

Noah pinched the bridge of his nose. "Please don't tell me he was run off the road by another vehicle."

"Nope. Word is, after retiring, the old sheriff enjoyed fishing. He drowned early one morning in a large fishing pond in Jackson Hole. The coroner ruled it a heart attack."

"This just keeps getting better and better," Noah mumbled to himself and closed his eyes. "This whole thing stinks to high heaven."

"Agreed." There was a long moment of silence.

"You know, buddy, you can bow out at any time and scuttle on back to Texas."

Noah didn't say anything and Alex sighed. "I didn't think so. This woman mean that much to you?"

Noah kept quiet. *Did she?*

"I'll send the report to your email. You can access it on your phone."

Noah's grip tightened on the phone. "Thanks."

"No problem." And then Alex was gone.

Noah lay on his back and stared at the old beaded ceiling of his room. He didn't owe Abby anything. They hadn't even known each other that long. He could go back to Blessing and let Alex handle the case. But everything in him rebelled against that idea as he visualized Abby running out of her house in her pink heart pajamas. And the kiss they had shared, the kiss he was trying to forget.

He punched in a number. He needed to touch base with his son. Dylan always lifted his spirits. Noah had been angry with God for a long time for taking his wife, but he did have Dylan, and for that he would be forever grateful.

Abby woke up and shoved Bates out of her face. The dog loved to lick her awake every morning. She had woken several times during the night, and each time her dog had had his throat draped across hers. It was a Malinois trait, or so the breeder said. But after having lived with him, she understood it was a protective maneuver that showed the animal knew she was upset. And she *was* upset.

The previous night flooded her mind. Who was the guy who had visited her room? She hadn't gotten a good look at his face. He appeared to be the same height and build as the man from the crash scene and the hospital. Could it be also be the person who'd saved them during the explosion at Grammy's house?

A lump crawled up her throat. Could he possibly be her brother?

The man had warned her not to trust anyone—not even Noah—but after praying for what seemed an eternity, Abby felt in her heart that she should tell Noah about her nocturnal visitor. She laughed—and it felt great—when Bates jumped off the bed and ran into the bathroom to drink water out of the toilet. Normally, she wouldn't allow that, but the poor fellow had to be hungry and thirsty. Probably needed to go outside, too.

A sense of relief and rightness flowed through her as she scrambled out of bed and slipped into her robe. She would see to Bates and then tell Noah everything. He might have distanced himself from her, but she would be mature and do the right thing. Bates's paws clicked on the old wooden floor when he heard her get out of bed. Adoring eyes followed her movements as she washed her face, dressed, brushed her teeth and combed her hair.

"Come on, baby boy. Let's get you outside before you have an accident."

She didn't bother with a leash and they hurried down the stairs. Noah was waiting at the bottom with a steaming cup of coffee in one hand. Those electric-blue eyes were stone cold and his jaw was squared, but things would change once she shared everything.

"Morning, Noah. We'll be right back."

He looked at the dog in understanding and gave a brisk nod. "I'll go out with you."

The cold outside air pierced her thin clothes and Abby's breath caught in her throat. Bates did his business and she hurried them back inside. Noah was right behind them and his predatory gaze tracked her as she poured herself a cup of coffee. The warm liquid almost made her purr in appreciation. She placed the coffee on the small table, sat down and looked at Noah.

"Noah, I—"

He held up a hand. "Don't say anything. First, I checked on Mrs. Denton several times throughout the night. Right now, she's sleeping soundly and I want to talk to you before she wakes."

Abby smiled. "Praise the Lord."

Noah grimaced. "Don't praise the Lord just yet."

Bates ignored the humans, munching happily away at the food Noah had put out for him.

Abby was bursting to clear the air. "Noah, I have to tell you—"

"Quiet!" The shouted command took Abby off guard and she waited as he drew in a deep breath.

"Alex Ridenhour called this morning. You know the accident report that burned in the fire here in Jackson?" She nodded. Where was he going with this?

"Simon found a file buried deep within the FBI system. It was on your parents."

A sense of foreboding crept over Abby. "Why would the FBI have a file on my parents' car crash if it was ruled an accident?"

If anything, Noah's jaw squared even more. "Bottom line? There's something bad going on here."

Abby took several deep breaths and centered herself. She could do this. If her parents had been murdered, she had to hold herself together so they could find the truth.

Bates whined and she rubbed his head.

"Please sit down." He was less intimidating when seated.

He sat and she slid into a chair across from him.

"I get the feeling that you're holding something back. If I'm to help you, I need to know everything."

He was right, and she had already come to that conclusion herself. "Last night, I had a visitor."

His lips tightened. "Go on."

"I think it might have been the guy from the crash scene, the one I saw in the hospital and the man who saved us after the explosion at Grammy's."

"You didn't get a good look at him?"

"There was a little light filtering through the window from the streetlamp, but no, I didn't get a clear look."

"You should have called me." His voice sounded grim and guarded.

Abby shrugged. She couldn't even explain it to herself. "Something told me to get as much information as I could. I had my gun trained on him, and Bates would have attacked if I had given the word. Anyway, I didn't get much information. He told me it was safer if I didn't know who he is. He advised me to hide, permanently. He said I shouldn't trust anyone—" she looked at him "—including you. He said the people after me have far-reaching arms, including local law enforcement and high-placed politicians. I asked if they were after him, too. Said that maybe we could help. He told me they, whoever 'they' are, think he's dead."

NINETEEN

Noah ached to trust her with every fiber of his being. And it did help that she'd come clean about the previous night, but her late-night visitor only raised more questions. Avoiding the trust issue that had built a wall between them, he zeroed in on the intruder. "Is that everything he said?"

"That's when you started banging on my door."

"From what he said, it sounds like he faked his own death. If we had a time frame, we could make a list of all high-profile deaths."

She shivered, and Noah felt a surge of protectiveness but pushed it away.

"You think it's really high profile?"

Bates left his food bowl and settled on the floor at Abby's side. Noah was truly impressed with the dog. He appeared to sense Abby's every mood. "From what the guy said—if he's telling the truth and this isn't a smoke screen and a way for whoever is after you to get close to you—then, yes, I'd have to assume the people responsible are high profile. There's also the sealed FBI file to consider. Someone has to be very rich and powerful, with connections in high places to have made that happen. We have to think big."

A myriad of emotions passed over Abby's face—frustration, confusion, anger—and Noah felt helpless to make them disappear. It was not a feeling he was accustomed to.

"That coffee I smell?" Mrs. Denton asked from the doorway before slowly shuffling into the room, breaking the mind-numbing tension.

Both Abby and Noah stood, but he reached their temporary landlady first and took her elbow, guiding her to a chair.

Abby filled a cup with steaming coffee. "Cream or sugar, Mrs. Denton?"

"No, dear, I take mine black and strong."

Abby handed her the cup and sat beside her. Noah wondered how he could even think of mistrusting Abby as she took Mrs. Denton's arthritic hand in her own.

"I bet you're sore this morning. My grandmother has a salve she always used on my scrapes and bruises when I was a kid."

The older lady smiled and her eyes drifted in remembrance. "I've doctored scrapes and bruises a time or two, myself." She refocused on Abby. "But that's a story for another time. I remembered something this morning when I woke up."

Abby pushed away from the table. "Let me make you some breakfast and then we can talk."

Mrs. Denton grabbed her hand. "I'll eat later. This is important. You never know when God might call me home and you need to know this."

Noah almost laughed at the horrified expression on Abby's face. "Do you need to go to the hospital? Did those men hurt you more than you admitted last night?"

Abby's voice rose in volume and Mrs. Denton held

up a defensive hand. "Pipe down, young lady. I'll probably outlive you all."

Abby looked as if she wanted to argue, but plopped back down in her seat.

"With so much going on last night, I forgot about Sandra Wentworth. She's the local librarian. Your parents pretty much kept to themselves, but I remember your mother loved to read and she visited the library a few times while they were here. Anyway, one day I saw your mama and Sandra riding in a car together. It was strange, because your parents were always together, with the boy, when they were here. They seldom went out to eat and took most of their meals here at the B and B."

Noah's sixth sense kicked in. "What did you think when you saw them together in the car?"

Mrs. Denton smiled. "I thought it was nice that Mary Beauchamp had a new friend. You might want to talk to Sandra and see what she has to say."

"Thank you," Abby said, then looked at him. "Noah, Mrs. Denton can't be left alone, not after what happened last night."

At least he had this covered. "Sheriff Hoyt isn't taking any chances. He's sending someone over to stay until this situation is resolved."

"He better not send that nosy Patty Hatfield over here. That woman—"

The doorbell rang and interrupted Mrs. Denton's tirade. Noah jumped to his feet and removed himself from the line of fire. "I'll get it."

Checking the holster at the back of his jeans, he peered through the peephole. A little old lady glared back at him, so close to the tiny glass he could almost count her wrinkles.

He opened the door and she sniffed. "Took you long enough." Without even saying hello, she marched past him as if she owned the place. Noah was afraid of World War Three breaking out because he had a sneaky feeling this was, indeed, Mrs. Hatfield.

Sparks were already flying between the two adversaries when he entered the kitchen. He almost laughed at the startled expression on Abby's face. He motioned her to follow him and she quickly scuttled out of the room.

"Ethan's deputy is watching out for them since I'm leaving the premises. He's in his patrol car outside. The sheriff just called a neighbor to be inside with Mrs. Denton since she has a slight head injury. He wanted someone with her at all times. Let's go pay Sandra Wentworth a visit."

Abby nodded and they grabbed their coats. Bates brought up the rear.

They left her dog in the car when they arrived at the library. The building was old, filled with endless shelves of books. The air had a musty odor, but Abby loved it. There were a few computers perched on one desk.

As they approached a pretty young woman at the front desk, Noah took the lead.

"Ma'am, we're looking for Sandra Wentworth."

The perky girl, who Abby guessed was somewhere in her early twenties, pointed toward an old staircase in the middle of the room. "Sure thing. Go up the stairs, first door on the right."

Side by side they climbed the wooden steps and Noah knocked on the door.

"Come in," a firm voice called.

Noah opened the door and they entered an office

that could have been featured in a historical painting. Everything was antique—tables, chairs, pictures. A woman who looked to be in her late fifties rose from behind a wooden desk with a beautiful patina. There were a few wrinkles around her smiling eyes, but she had beautiful skin. Her blond hair was streaked with a few strands of silver.

"Hello. Susie buzzed me and said you were coming up." She held out a hand, and Noah clasped it and shook. Abby followed suit, but when Sandra Wentworth faced Abby head-on, the woman gasped and turned an alarming shade of white. Abby held on to her hand. "Mrs. Wentworth, are you alright? Noah, fetch a glass of water."

The head librarian took a deep breath and some color returned. She pulled her hand away. "I—I'm fine. Please, have a seat."

Abby watched her carefully, but she seemed to steady herself.

"You're sure you're okay?"

Mrs. Wentworth's lips trembled. "Yes. Well, no, maybe not." She stared at Abby. "You just, well, you look like someone I once knew."

Mrs. Wentworth straightened a pen on her desk, and when she looked back up, a mask of wariness had fallen over her face. In a crisp tone, she said, "Why don't you tell me who you are and why you're here?"

Noah started to speak, but Abby had suddenly had enough. She was at the end of her rope and she wanted answers. "I'll tell you why we're here. Someone has broken into my house several times. I've been shot at. My car has been run off the road, and Noah and I barely escaped the explosion that destroyed my grandmother's house. And that's after someone roughed up my grandmother and put her in the hospital. Mrs. Denton told us you were friends with my mother—Mary Beauchamp—and we need to know what happened all those years ago when they died in a car crash."

Abby snapped her mouth shut, immediately feeling contrite as a stricken expression fell across Mrs. Wentworth's face.

Ashamed and embarrassed, Abby lifted a hand, then let it drop back into her lap. "I'm sorry. It's just that my life has spiraled out of control and I don't know how to fix it. Please, let me start over. My name is Abby Mayfield and this is Noah Galloway. He's the sheriff in a Texas town called Blessing. I teach piano and I'm a choir director." Abby took a deep breath. "Mrs. Wentworth, someone is trying to kill me and I don't have a clue who would do such a thing."

Abby held her breath as the librarian studied them a moment. "I'd like to see some identification, please."

Both of them pulled out their driver's licenses, and Noah added his sheriff's ID, then they passed them over. She put on a pair of reading glasses and studied them in detail. Finally, she handed them back and propped both elbows on her desk. "Driver's licenses can be forged, but I believe you because you're the spitting image of your mother."

Abby's heart raced. Finally! "So you knew her? You knew my mama?"

Noah injected a question. "Why the caution, Mrs. Wentworth?"

"Please, call me Sandra. *Mrs. Wentworth* is a mouthful."

They shared a stilted laugh, but Abby was on pins and needles. What did Sandra know?

"And call us Abby and Noah," Abby responded in kind.

Sandra nodded and leaned back in her chair. "Are you sure someone is trying to kill you?"

Noah answered for Abby. "No doubt whatsoever."

Sandra gave a jerky nod. "I'll tell you what I know, which, I'll warn you, is very little. Your mother was extremely secretive."

Her heart lodged in her throat, Abby nodded. "Anything you share is much appreciated."

"Your mother visited the library the one time they came to Jackson and the cutest boy accompanied her. I asked if the child was her son. She got the strangest look on her face, almost fearful, and peered over her shoulder, as if afraid someone was watching her. I asked if anything was wrong, and she relaxed and laughed. She said they were babysitting for a relative so the parents could take a long-deserved break. I thought maybe I had misread her. We talked for quite a while and had a lot in common, a love of books being one of them, but the last time she came by during their visit…"

Abby found herself leaning forward in her chair. "The last time?"

Sandra lifted eyes full of remorse. "The last time I saw your mother alive, the only way I can describe her attitude was one of fear mixed with excitement. She came to say goodbye, said they'd never return to Jackson. I was disturbed, to say the least. She warned me not to let anyone in Jackson know we had close acquaintance, and if anyone came to town asking questions about them, to deny I knew her, even if it was the police. She said it was too dangerous. Not to trust anyone."

An eerie, creepy feeling stole over Abby and she turned to Noah. "That's the same thing the man said last night. Don't trust anyone."

Noah kept his eyes trained on Sandra. "What about the boy? Was he with her?"

Sandra shook her head. "He wasn't with her that last time she stopped by the library."

She looked at Noah, long and hard. "They didn't have an accident, did they?"

"No, Mrs. Wentworth. We now believe they were forced off the road."

Abby worried for the woman when her face went white again, but Sandra held herself together. "I honored Mary's request. I've never told a soul, until you two, that we were acquainted."

Noah nodded. "Probably wise. Was there anything else?"

Sandra shook her head, a sad look in her eyes. "No, but, Abby, I'm sorry. I wish I could have done something to prevent such a horrible tragedy."

A tear in her eye, Abby stood and Noah followed suit. "It sounds to me like you were a good friend when my mama needed one. Thank you for being open with us."

Sandra stood, rounded the desk and hugged Abby. "Please be careful. I'll be praying for your safety and that you find the answers you're looking for."

Abby hugged her back, and she and Noah were silent, lost in their own thoughts, as they left the library. When they stepped outside, the first thing Abby heard was Bates. She jerked her gaze to the car where the dog was doing his best to squeeze out of the window they'd left cracked open. At her side, Noah stiffened, grabbed her arm and pulled her into a nosedive behind the rear of the car.

As her shoulder took the brunt of the fall, Abby heard a ping similar to the one at the church. Someone was shooting at them.

TWENTY

His gun already in his hand, Noah scrambled to a crouched position and, with his back to the bumper, made sure Abby was out of the line of fire. She sat on the ground, hugging the back of the vehicle.

Her wide, startled eyes made him want to crush something, or someone. Her cross-body purse was still in position. "You have your cell phone in there?"

She nodded.

"Call 911 and tell them to notify Sheriff Hoyt. After you've done that, go to the other side of the car and crawl inside with Bates. Stay there until you hear sirens."

Noah was impressed when she took a quick breath and pulled herself together. "Where are you going?"

Her courage strengthened his resolve. He was tired of being on the defensive. It was time to get some answers. "I'm going hunting."

He sounded hard and cold, but that's how he felt. He turned and took a quick look around the bumper of the car. All clear as far as he could tell. Without looking back, he took off after the shooter.

As he hustled around the opposite side of the library from where he thought the shots had been fired, his mind became a whirlwind of activity. He grimaced as he rounded the building, but for the first time in a long time, he said a quick prayer for safety. He had a sneaking suspicion that God had given him something besides Dylan to live for. He had to get his head back in the game. The people after Abby were playing for keeps, and they'd be happy to get rid of Noah, making it easier to get close to Abby, because nobody could, or would, protect her like he would.

Crouched low, with both hands on the gun in front of him, he looked up and checked the roofline as he ran along beside the old brick wall of the library. The building was only two stories high and the bullet had come from ground level, but that didn't mean there wasn't a second shooter. Two people had visited Mrs. Denton.

He took a quick look around the back corner of the building and jerked back as another bullet chipped off a piece of brick. The bullet came from the woods behind the library. Too close for comfort. The perpetrators were getting bolder. He needed to catch one of them for interrogation purposes. They didn't have enough clues to go on and things were escalating. This was his chance. He shouldn't go after them without backup, but he wanted Abby safe.

He took another quick glance around the corner. Nobody shot at him, and he was getting ready to take off toward the woods when a vicious bark filled the air.

Noah immediately switched gears and raced back to the car, castigating himself all the way. What if a second person had backtracked and gone after Abby? He'd never forgive himself if something happened to her. He heard sirens blaring and Sheriff Hoyt brought his patrol car to a shuddering halt, jumping out with his weapon drawn as Noah rounded the corner of the building. Hoyt canvassed the area with his own gun held in front of him, checking all around before concluding it was safe.

Hoyt lowered his weapon and they both approached the car. His heart in his throat, Noah allowed himself to breathe a sigh of relief when Abby threw the back door open and both woman and dog scrambled out of the vehicle. She made a beeline toward him. He released an *oomph* when she rocketed into his chest and wrapped her arms around his waist.

His body sagged in relief. She was okay. He held her tight for a few seconds before pulling back, distancing himself.

Sheriff Hoyt cleared his throat. "I suggest we take it to the station so y'all can tell me what happened," he drawled. "The shooter, or shooters, are still at large."

In less than ten minutes, Noah followed Abby through the police station doors. He couldn't believe he'd allowed whoever was after Abby to get the drop on him. All the more reason to distance himself from his attraction to her. He had to keep his head in the game and stay vigilant. Her life was at stake.

Hoyt sat behind his desk, and Abby took a seat next to Noah. Noah gave the sheriff a quick but accurate account of the shooting.

Before Hoyt had a chance to ask any questions, his deputy came careening into the room, almost stumbling in his haste.

"Sheriff," he exclaimed. "You gotta come outside right now."

Sheriff Hoyt sighed, much like Noah did around Cooper, and Noah hid a smile.

"What is it, Peter?"

Noah could almost see the sparks of excitement bouncing off the deputy.

"It's Ned. He's in front of the station. He caught one of the shooters."

Noah's gaze sharpened as he looked at Hoyt. "Who's Ned?"

Hoyt shook his head and grabbed his coat off the back of his chair. "I'll explain later."

Noah and Abby followed him out the door and through the police station. The cold air hit first, but he soon forgot the freezing temperatures when he caught sight of a man trussed up with a heavy rope, sitting on the sidewalk in front of the building. He couldn't speak due to the rag stuffed into his mouth. Not that he wasn't trying.

But the most intriguing aspect of the odd situation was the bear of a man holding the criminal upright by his coat collar. The man was big. Noah estimated him to be well over six and a half feet tall. Hair covered most of his face, and he had piercing green eyes. Eyes that held far more intelligence than his appearance suggested. His clothes consisted of faded jeans and a heavy fleece jacket. Hiking boots covered his feet.

Abby crowded close behind Noah and he almost smiled at her not-so-subtle eavesdropping technique.

"Bear Man," she whispered, nicknaming the man, and Noah choked back a laugh.

Sheriff Hoyt spoke. "Ned, haven't seen you around in a while."

Noah wanted him to get on with it. He prayed the trussed-up man was one of the shooters.

Bear Man—or rather, Ned—grunted. "Been busy." He jerked his prisoner by the collar. "I believe this belongs to you."

After that short announcement, Ned turned on his boot heel and left. Noah watched him disappear into the woods, which led straight up a desolate mountain. Blessing had a few odd people, but this guy was an entity of his own. Noah also noticed his movements as he walked away. Agile and smooth. This was no ordinary mountain man. Noah had a ton of questions about him, but the sheriff motioned Peter over and they started cutting the captive loose as the deputy read him his rights.

As soon as they removed the gag, he spit on the ground and snarled at all of them. "I want to talk to my lawyer. You people around here are nuts."

Noah moved in front of Abby as she took a few steps back. The captive had a New York accent. Had he followed them all the way to Jackson? Had he tried to kill her?

Anger flashed hot and crushed Abby's common sense. By now, Sheriff Hoyt had cuffs on the prisoner. Avoiding Noah's grasping hand, she marched right in front of him and stuck a finger in the man's face.

"I better not find out you had anything to do with hurting my grandmother."

He opened his mouth, no doubt to blast her, but Bates came alongside her and released a fierce growl that would make a grown person wet his pants. The man took a step back and Abby felt like snarling, herself.

Noah grabbed her arm and pulled her away from the guy. Sheriff Hoyt guided the man forward.

"You have to reign in that steel-magnolia thing you have going, Abby," Noah said in a low voice.

She sighed. "I know. It's just that…"

"It's okay. I understand. Maybe we'll get some answers now."

Hope—the first she'd had since this whole mess started—filled her. "Do you think he'll talk?"

Noah took her hand and followed the procession into the station. "I'm sure he'll lawyer up, but we'll do our best." He grinned. "I do know a few interrogation techniques."

Abby breathed a lungful of cold air before entering the station. Hoyt and his prisoner had disappeared. Peter was waiting for Noah. "The sheriff's locking him up. He'll be back in a minute."

Noah nodded and led her to a bench lining the wall. She sat down and he squatted in front of her. "Why don't you get some coffee and stay here while we talk to this guy?"

She wanted to argue, but Noah raised a brow. Somehow, in the short amount of time they'd spent together, he could already interpret her reactions.

"Fine, I'll stay put."

He met Hoyt halfway down the hall. Abby watched as they disappeared into the back of the building.

She drank three cups of horrible, strong coffee, paced, got a snack out of the vending machine, paced some more, went to the ladies' room and kept walking back and forth across the worn-out linoleum. Bates sat on the floor and watched her with alert eyes that missed nothing. When Sheriff Hoyt and Noah came back down the hall, she searched his face. He didn't look pleased, but neither did he look upset. He motioned for her to follow them and they ended up back in Hoyt's office.

The sheriff sat down behind his desk, and Abby and Noah took the seats facing him.

"Well?" she asked.

Hoyt nodded at Noah and Noah explained, "At first he wanted to lawyer up, but I told him a deal might be on the table if he cooperated."

Abby didn't much care for making deals with a hardened criminal, but she kept her mouth shut. This was what Noah had been trained to do.

"He admitted they were trying to kill you. He and his partner have been hiding in the mountains, waiting for an opportunity to strike."

Abby grimaced at hearing the stark truth, but she shored up her courage. "Go on."

Noah grinned. "They almost froze to death. There were two of them, but his partner called it quits after roughing up Mrs. Denton. He went back to New York. The guy we arrested owes some dangerous people a lot of money and he decided to follow through. Unfortunately, his instructions and payments were dropped at a neutral location. He has no idea who hired him."

"Do you believe him?"

"Yes, I do. I've interviewed many people, and remember, we now believe this is high profile. If someone in a position of power is calling the shots, they'll make sure nothing can be traced back to them."

Abby wanted to weep, but she sniffed and regained her equilibrium.

Noah stood and held out a hand to Sheriff Hoyt. "Once again, I appreciate your help."

Hoyt stood and shook his hand. "Anytime. Let me know how everything pans out."

Abby was curious. "It sounds like we're leaving. Where are we going? What about Ned? What's his story?"

"The sheriff and I both agree, since the killers were likely hired in New York, our answers lie there."

Hoyt answered her question about Ned. "Ned showed up about three years ago, bought an entire mountain and built a cabin. He comes into town once a month to buy supplies, but keeps to himself for the most part. He has returned a couple of lost hikers during that time. As long as he doesn't cause trouble, he can do what he wants. It's a free country."

Abby could tell the sheriff wasn't satisfied with the limited amount of information he had on the man, but that was his problem. She had enough of her own.

"It was nice to meet you, Sheriff."

He nodded and they left. The bracing air smacked her in the face as she loaded Bates into the back of the car and climbed into the passenger seat. Noah rounded the front of the vehicle and got behind the wheel.

"What now?" she asked.

Before he could answer, his phone rang. "Simon, you got something for me?"

She couldn't stop the skipped beat of her heart. She was coming to realize hope was a very fragile thing. Noah opened the glove compartment and grabbed a pad and pen.

"Go ahead."

Abby watched as he wrote a number down. It started with the letters *C-A-M* followed by the numbers three-six-six and her heart leaped again.

"Good work, Simon. Yes, I'll buy you a steak dinner when this is over."

Noah laughed as he put the phone away. "That kid is an empty bucket. If he ate six meals a day, he'd still be hungry."

Abby was about to bust. "Noah!"

He grinned and put the car in gear. "We're picking up our luggage and heading back to New York."

TWENTY-ONE

"Noah Galloway, you better share this instant if you know what's good for you." Her tone was teasing, but there was steel behind the request.

He started the engine and put the car in Drive. "Simon researched all the cars with tags starting with *C-A-M.* The one I just wrote down raised a red flag because it's owned by a corporation."

Invisible, electric energy came off her in waves. "Well, what's the name of the cooperation?"

He hated to burst her bubble, but this was a good, solid lead. "Simon says it's a dummy corporation, but it gives us a good place to start."

She deflated, and he shifted in his seat, facing her after pulling in to Mrs. Denton's bed-and-breakfast parking area and cutting the engine. "Abby, listen to me. This is a great lead. Simon is a whiz at this. We'll track the corporate owner of this tag. It's only a matter of time. They can use shell corporations, but we will find them."

Her eyes were filled with such faith it made him want to conquer the world.

"I trust you, Noah. We'll find them. Let's load up

and say goodbye to Mrs. Denton. I'll make flight plans while you pack."

Noah felt bad for Abby, even though she insisted she wasn't tired. Her drooping shoulders and the faint crescent moons under her eyes said otherwise.

After saying their goodbyes to Mrs. Denton, and what seemed like a long flight to New York, they checked into a different hotel this time and grabbed a bite to eat before trekking back to the FBI offices.

They had crisscrossed the country several times, and he was feeling the effects, too. Noah had tried to talk her into taking a nap, but she said she was sick and tired of this mess. She wanted her life back, and the only way to do that was to find answers.

He agreed, so they kept moving.

Everyone was waiting in Director Henry Wilson's office when they arrived. After a short greeting period, they took seats.

Wilson started the meeting. "I hear you saw a little action in Jackson Hole."

Noah nodded. "Yes, sir, but we handled it."

"I'm having the prisoner transferred to our jurisdiction. Sheriff Hoyt was very helpful."

"He's a good man."

Abby half listened as drowsiness threatened to overtake her, but the numbers Noah had written down while they were in the car in Jackson Hole kept running through her mind. CAM366. It nagged at her.

Someone shook her arm. "Abby, you okay?"

It was Noah and he sounded concerned. She forced a smile. "I'm fine, but…"

"But what?"

"Those letters and numbers? The ones on the license tag?"

"What about them?"

"They… What if…?"

Exasperation replaced his concern. "What if they what?"

And it came to her like an answered prayer from God. "Give me the phone."

Everyone in the room sent Noah pitying glances.

"Abby—"

She sat straight up, electrified energy pumping through her now. "The phone. Give it to me."

Noah looked at her askance but started digging his cell phone out of his pocket.

Now she became exasperated. "No. Not that one. I need a landline."

Director Wilson grabbed the cordless phone off his desk and handed it to her. "Here you go."

She knew everyone thought she had lost it, but she didn't care. She stared at the numbers on the handset, trying different letter combinations. "The numbers three-six-six could equal *D-O-N*," she mumbled under her breath.

"Abby, what are you talking about?" Noah's words were laced with worry, but she ignored him. She was on to something. She could feel it.

"Simon, do you have your laptop with you?" she asked, terrified she might be wrong, but praying she was right.

Simon reached down beside his chair and grinned when he lifted his computer. "Never go anywhere without it."

"Good, please type in *C-A-M-D-O-N*."

"Abby—"

"Wait," she told Noah. "Just wait." She focused on Simon as he typed in the word.

He looked up and grinned. "How did you figure it out?"

She grinned back. "The keypad on the phone. *D* is the number three, *O* and *N* are the number six. *C-A-M-three-six-six*. Camdon. I tried different combinations, but this one jumped out at me."

"Please, if someone would fill me in, I would appreciate it," Director Wilson demanded more than asked.

Simon turned his computer around so everyone could see the screen. "I ran the original plate and it's owned by a shell corporation. Your combination spells *Camdon*, which could possibly stand for Camdon International. It's a huge corporation based right here in New York, and the owner's heir died recently."

The room erupted into chaos with everyone talking at once. Wilson raised a hand. "One person at a time, people."

Abby's heart palpitated. This had to be the information they needed to solve the mystery surrounding her. She didn't think she could take much more. *Dear Lord, please let this be a clue that will lead us to the truth.*

Noah stared at her, his eyes full of surprise and approval. "How did you come up with that?"

Abby grinned. "God gave it to me."

He nodded slowly and her heart gave a giant leap. Maybe all this had happened so Noah could find his way back to God. If that were true, it would be worth every dangerous moment she'd lived through.

Everyone in the room laughed and Abby looked at Director Wilson. "What did you say?"

His eyes danced. "I said I ought to hire you. You'd make a good code solver for the FBI."

Totally humbled, Abby flushed at the praise. "Thank you, but I've already got a job as a choir director and we've yet to prove the tag belongs to Camdon International."

Wilson started issuing commands. "Simon—"

Simon popped out of his chair, laptop in hand and headed for the door. "I'll get Franny on it right away, sir."

Abby girded her courage and took a deep breath. Avoiding eye contact with Noah, she boldly made her statement. "Sir? Director Wilson?"

He turned sharply. "Yes?"

Abby squirmed in her seat and cleared her throat. "If the plate does belong to Camdon International, I would like to offer my services as bait, if need be."

Noah's entire body stiffened in the chair beside her, but she was determined. She wanted this to end.

"Sir." Noah jumped in before his boss could speak, "As you well know, it's FBI policy never to use a civilian as bait."

Director Wilson's eyes crinkled when he smiled at Abby. "Ms. Mayfield, I appreciate the offer. It's very brave of you, but Galloway's correct in saying we would never place a civilian in the line of fire."

All of a sudden, fatigue weighed down on her and she yawned.

Noah caught the movement and stood. "We're heading back to the hotel. Call if you need us."

Everyone in the room mumbled a goodbye and they were on their way. In the car, Noah roused her after reaching the parking enclosure at the hotel. "Abby. We're here. Let's get some rest. They'll call if anything happens."

She nodded sleepily and he guided her into the elevator and to her room. After locking the dead bolt behind him, he moved to the connecting door. "This door is unlocked. Yell if you need me, but we should be safe. We're on an upper floor and there are no balconies."

She waited until the door closed. Once again, she fell to bed fully clothed. She heard Bates drinking out of the toilet and reminded herself to put out his water bowl as soon as she awakened. After drinking his fill, he climbed in beside her, his warm body making her feel secure.

In a deep slumber, Abby swatted at her ear. At first she thought it was the fur from Bates's ear tickling her. He always slept with his head next to hers.

She reached over to snuggle next to him, but a deep, low whisper penetrated her sleep.

"Your dog's not here and you need to wake up. Now!"

She recognized that voice and her eyes popped open. She was wide awake now. She tried to yell for Noah, but the man placed a hand over her mouth.

"Listen." There was urgency in his voice. "They're coming after you and we have to get out of here. They'll kill us both. Can I lift my hand? Promise you won't scream?"

Abby weighed her options. If the guy wanted to kill her, he could have done so while she was asleep. She nodded in the affirmative and he slowly lifted his hand.

"Where's my dog? Where's Bates?" was her first question.

He pointed toward the bathroom. "He was drinking water out of the toilet when I slipped in. I brought a rib bone just in case, threw it inside as a treat and closed the door before he could get out. I think he remembered me from your grandmother's house and that's why he isn't barking his head off."

She scrambled out of bed and threw her robe on before flying to the bathroom. Opening the door, she breathed a sigh of relief and knelt beside her protector and best friend. He was happily gnawing on the bone.

"Some guard dog you are," she said, and chuckled at the red sauce on his whiskers.

Looking over her shoulder, she shot a questioning glance at the man who had saved Noah from the fire at her grandmother's house. "How did you get in here?"

"I waited in the hall. Things are getting hot for the killers and I knew they'd make a move soon. Abby, they're powerful and loaded with money. A hotel employee opened your dead bolt while you were asleep. That's how I got in, and I'm sure the employee was paid to do so. You have to hurry because they'll be here soon. We have to go."

As unobtrusively as possible, she cast a glance toward Noah's door. It was unlocked. She gauged the distance between herself and the door. She could make a run for it or she could yell. The man must have realized her intent. He crossed the room in a flash and knelt beside her. She peered into a face so similar to her own, her heart ached. "Are you my brother?"

Deep sorrow filled his eyes. "I'll answer all your questions later, but you have to trust me. We have to leave now."

"But Noah can help us."

A shuttered expression covered his face. "Stay with him or leave with me. It's your choice. This thing reaches high places, and I'm positive there are paid informants within the FBI. Maybe your Noah isn't one of them, but his coworkers or boss might be. Abby, they'll kill him if they get the chance."

And those words prompted her into action. She'd never do anything that would put Noah at risk. She stood and faced the man head-on. "How do I know I can trust you?"

Indecision flitted across his face until he appeared to come to a decision. "My name is Sam Camdon. I'm your brother."

Abby closed her eyes in prayer. When she opened them, she nodded firmly. "I'll go with you, but I'm leaving a note for Noah, so he'll know what's going on." She turned to Bates. She didn't want Noah or her dog killed. "Bates, you stay here, baby, and stay quiet."

She got to her feet. With no idea what situations they might face, she decided to leave Bates in the bathroom. "I'll leave Bates here. Noah will take care of him."

"Fine, but hurry. We're running out of time."

Abby rushed over to the desk by the window. Her hands shook as she gathered pen and paper. Just as she was finishing writing the note, the lock on the door rattled and was quickly jimmied. Two burly men stepped in, guns drawn, and closed the door behind them. Her brother must have forgotten to reset the dead bolt.

Abby opened her mouth to yell, but the barrel of the gun swinging in her direction had her snapping her mouth shut.

"Scream and I'll kill you both. Now, walk nice and slowly toward the door. One wrong move and you're both dead."

TWENTY-TWO

Noah awoke to a raucous noise coming from Abby's room. He heard barking, snarling and growling. It sounded like the Malinois was repeatedly hurling himself against a wall. Fear for Abby threatened to immobilize him, but he scrambled out of bed and grabbed his gun off the night-stand. He took a deep breath, centering himself, and placed a hand on the doorknob. He was ready to spring into action.

He threw the door open, took a two-hand hold on the Glock and visually swept the room. Frantic, he checked the bathroom and found Bates, but Abby was nowhere to be seen. The distraught dog followed him from the bathroom to the hall door. It swung open at his touch.

His heart felt as if it was going to beat out of his chest as he sat on the end of the bed. He had failed Abby. Was she alive? The thought almost brought him to his knees. Noah closed his eyes, and for the first time since Dylan's mother died, he fully opened his heart. "God, I beg You." He raised his voice. "Please let Abby be alive. Show me where to find her."

He had prayed for Sonya to live, but she had died, anyway. Would God listen this time?

A cold nose nudged his hand and he looked down. "Bates, what happened? How did they get past you?"

The dog's soulful eyes reflected heartbreak and abashment, much the way Noah felt, but then the dog tugged at his pants leg.

"What is it, boy?" He stood and Bates raced over to the desk sitting in front of the window. A pad and pen lay side by side and his insides froze when he read the message.

Noah, the blond guy is my brother, and he's here. His name is Sam Camdon. He wants me to leave with him. I wanted to wake you, but he said these people will kill you, and I believe him. I left Bates in the bathroom because I was afraid whoever wants me dead might kill him if they catch up with us. It appears they paid a hotel employee to unlock my dead bolt. Noah—

A jagged line started at the last word and ended at the bottom of the page. They had her. They'd stolen her right out from under his nose. A fierce surge of protectiveness raced through him. He looked at the dog. "Let's go find Abby."

The dog stood by the door, his muscular body quivering, ready to roll.

"Let me get dressed and we're outta here."

As he stepped into his room, his cell, sitting on the nightstand, rang. He put it on speakerphone while throwing on his clothes. "Not now, Simon. They have her. They have Abby."

"Then you need to know this. Abby was right. After sifting through numerous shell corporations, the car tag belongs to Camdon International."

Noah had no idea where they'd taken Abby and her brother, so he decided to go to the top of the company. "Who's in charge of Camdon International?" He heard Simon typing at warp speed.

"By the way, the blond guy in the police sketch is Sam Camdon. From what I can ascertain, he tried to fake his death."

Impatience made Noah snap, "I need to know who's in charge of Camdon International."

Simon ignored his outburst. "The old man's name is Lincoln Camdon. I have to give it to him, he built the company from scratch."

"Give me the address for the New York headquarters."

Simon rattled off the address and Noah memorized it as he and Bates ran out the door and into the hallway. "Tell Alex to meet me there."

"You got it."

A chill racked Abby's body as she and Sam were shoved into a small, cold room. The door clanged shut behind them and she raced back to it and rattled the knob.

"That won't do any good. Even if you get the door open, I'm sure there are guards posted outside." He sounded resigned to his fate.

Abby whirled around and got her first good look at her brother. His short, mussed blond hair and brown eyes reminded her so much of her mother she wanted to cry, but she wouldn't, because they were going to escape. The mere thought of dying brought a fierce surge of love in her heart for Noah. *Why now, Lord, when I might not make it out of this alive?* She had just fallen in love and discovered she had a brother. She took a deep, fierce breath. She refused to die. She had too much to live for.

She marched over to Sam and pointed a finger in his face. "Do you believe in God?"

Confusion spread over his face. "What?"

"I asked if you believe in God. It's a simple question."

He shrugged his shoulders. "I believe in a supreme being. Why?"

Abby rolled her eyes. She should have been terrified out of her mind, given the circumstances, but God was giving her strength. It flowed through her entire being like a strong, roaring waterfall. "Because believing in God is everything, and if you want to get out of this alive, you better start praying."

A hint of hope lit his eyes.

"Now, I want answers, and I mean everything. The whole story."

Sam's lips curved upward. "You're a bossy little thing."

"I'm a choir director and a piano teacher. Of course I'm bossy. Start at the beginning. I have to know everything if we're going to get out of this mess."

"Yes, ma'am." His grin faded. "Before you were born, our parents had a son. Me."

Abby drew in a sharp breath, even though the proof sat right in front of her.

"Our grandfather, Lincoln Camdon, and our father never got along. Lincoln is a tyrant of the worst sort. He wanted his son to follow in his footsteps, but our dad was averse to dealing in the shady side of business. Not that Lincoln ever crossed the line far enough to alert the Feds, but he did unsavory things to get what he wanted. From what my nanny explained to me when I was old enough to understand, when our mother was pregnant with you, the old man claimed me as his heir since his own son failed to fall in line."

Abby sat down next to him on the only bare cot in the room. "That's horrible."

"Yeah, well, it gets worse. Dear old Grandpa put several things in motion to make it look like our mother was going insane. He threatened to have her institutionalized if they didn't agree to take the new baby and leave me with him. Said he'd sue for custody of both children if they didn't agree."

Righteous indignation and a big dose of fury infused Abby and she shot off the cot. "The man's a monster."

"It gets worse. Through the years, I've pieced together what happened. My nanny told me part of it when I was young, and I gathered other pieces here and there. The way I understand it, our parents changed their names and went into hiding when you were a baby, hoping to get me back one day and have a secure location already in place where Lincoln couldn't find us, but unbeknownst to them, Lincoln hired a private investigator to follow them from the time they left.

"My nanny slipped me out three or four different times to see our parents. You were never there. I don't know why. Maybe they were afraid it would confuse you. I was ten years old when my nanny took me to Jackson Hole. Our parents told me they were taking me away with them, and I was so happy."

Abby's heart broke with every word he uttered. That one old man could cause such havoc was appalling.

"They made it sound like an adventure. I assume they thought they had outsmarted whoever had been following them. I was to go ahead with my nanny, and they would follow us later in their car, just in case someone had tailed the nanny to Jackson. They had decided on a destination, I'm not sure where, but about an hour after we left, two of Lincoln's bodyguards—thugs, really—pulled in front of our car and forced us to stop."

His eyes had a faraway look, but refocused on Abby. "They took the nanny and me back to New York and my nanny was dismissed. I didn't know until years later— Lincoln told me himself—that the men who stayed to watch our parents tried to get them to stop on the road, but they sped up and lost control of their car. They both died in the crash."

Abby slid over and wrapped her arms around her brother. "I'm so sorry for everything that happened to you."

He hugged her back, then pulled away and shrugged, as if it wasn't important, but it was. It was very important.

Abby processed everything he said, then asked, "But why did you fake your death if he wanted you to follow in his footsteps?"

Sam started pacing the room. "I wanted out. I wanted to live my own life, free of the greed and manipulation of the family."

Abby had to know something important before they went any further. "Did you have a happy childhood? Was he good to you?"

His lips tightened. "I did what I was told because he used you to blackmail me."

Shock rendered her speechless for a second. "What do you mean?"

"As a child, he told me something bad would happen to you—my only sister—if I didn't fall in line."

Deep sorrow filled her and Abby lowered her head. Two cold hands encased hers and she looked at her brother.

"Abby, you're my sister, and I loved you from afar. I grew up with everything money could buy. It wasn't so bad. If I was good, every week the old man would show me pictures he had taken of you and mom and dad before they were killed. I didn't want anything to happen to you. At first, I started following you, gathering the courage to introduce myself to you, and I knew something was very wrong when I spotted Julie and Walter in Blessing. I stayed in the background, trying to figure out what was going on. You saw me on that embankment after you were forced off the road. I had followed you to Mocksville and stayed well behind the vehicle that forced you off the road. I pulled onto a dirt road and hid my car, then made my way to the crash site. I had to be sure you were okay.

"I promised myself that I'd introduce myself to you and we would be the family we were meant to be."

"That God meant us to be," she whispered. "And we will have that chance," she said with firm resolve. "I have Noah, and now I have you. Nobody is going to take that away from me. Tell me about the scumbags who are willing to commit murder for money."

Noah and Alex flashed their identifications after entering the Camdon International building, with Bates accompanying them. After discovering that Lincoln Camdon was, indeed, in the country and in his office, Alex grabbed Noah's arm before entering the elevator of the mammoth building. "Let me handle this. You're running too hot and you're out of your jurisdiction."

Noah jerked his arm loose and stepped into the elevator, jabbing the button that would take them to the top floor. "Abby could be murdered at any minute. Don't talk to me about running hot."

Noah didn't miss the look of pity in Alex's eyes. His old partner already thought she was gone, but Noah refused to believe that. God wouldn't take love from him a second time. And he realized with startling clarity that he did love Abby. All crazy steel magnolia mixed with kindness and compassion and a host of wonderful attributes that he didn't have time to list right now. He was ready and willing to take a chance, hoping God would allow them more time together than he had with Noah and Sonya. With renewed resolve he exited the elevator, hoping with every fiber of his being that the perpetrators hadn't already killed Abby and her brother. That they preferred to make it look like an accident to throw off suspicion of murder, and that would give him some time.

A formidable-looking secretary rounded her desk and came running after them as Noah and Alex headed for the only massive double doors on the floor.

"You can't go in there!"

He ignored her and flung the doors open. Marching straight to the huge wooden desk, his gaze bore into the stately man sitting there, talking on the phone.

"Get off the phone. Now!"

The guy wore an expensive suit, and well-trimmed silver hair gave him a distinguished appearance. His eyebrows rose as he took in Noah and Alex. "I'll call you back," he said into the phone and hung up. He peered behind them. "Nancy, that will be all."

Lincoln Camdon's calmness only stirred Noah's anger.

"Security called and said you were on your way up. Can I offer you gentlemen something to drink?"

Noah gripped the edge of the desk with both hands

and leaned forward. "What you can do is tell me where Abby Mayfield is, and who's trying to kill her and why."

Either Camdon was a consummate actor, or he didn't have a clue, and if he didn't know where Abby was... Noah refused to go there. He would find her. Alive.

"I don't know what you're talking about." His words didn't match the worried expression on his face.

Noah growled and Bates mimicked him. Camdon shifted in his seat—the only sign of nervousness Noah could see. He had to get through to him. But how? And then it came to him.

"Your grandson, Sam Camdon, is alive."

Lincoln Camdon's face went parchment white and his lips trembled, but he held it together. "What proof do you have?"

"A note Abby left right before she was abducted. Now, I'll ask again, who wants Abby and her brother dead? Who's in line to inherit when you die if both of your grandchildren are gone?"

With a shaky hand, the older man pulled open a desk drawer and opened a bottle of pills. He popped one into his mouth and swallowed. He straightened his tie and squared his shoulders, as if this was a board meeting. Noah wanted to strangle the answers out of him.

"I have cancer. They've given me three months to live." Camdon raised eyes filled with regret. "I've done many things of which I'm not proud, and I'd like to see my grandchildren again before I die. Abby and Sam's two cousins inherit if there are no other living relatives."

Noah's patience was nearing an end. "Names?"

"Julie and Walter Camdon. My deceased brother's children."

Information ricocheted through Noah's brain and he connected the dots aloud. "Joanne Ferguson and Walter Fleming." He stared at Camdon. "They came to Blessing, Texas, and joined the choir. Abby's the choir director at the church." He was so close now, Noah could almost taste it. "Where would they take Abby and Sam?"

Camdon looked as if he was about to expire on the spot, but the lines on his forehead smoothed out. "His pet project. Walter's pet project. He's been working on something, but wouldn't tell me what it is. He wanted it to be a surprise."

Noah stood up straight. "Walter works for the company?"

Camdon also stood and rounded the desk. "Not after this. I know the warehouse he's using for the project. Let's go."

Noah didn't argue.

Abby's muscles tightened in readiness when the key turned in the lock. She nodded at Sam, who was hiding behind the door. It was a long shot, but it was the only plan she could come up with. The door swung open and Abby shook her head. "Why am I not surprised?"

Joanne Ferguson sashayed into the room. "Yes, it's me, and if your brother doesn't want you to die this minute, I suggest he move from behind the door."

Sam left his hiding place and came to stand beside her. Walter Fleming followed Joanne into the room, a gun in his hand.

"Hello, cousins," Sam drawled.

"These are the greedy cousins you were telling me about?"

"Now, now, my dear. You're supposed to be a sweet little choir director. Let's not go around slinging mud."

Anger grabbed Abby by the throat. She gritted her

teeth and balled her fists. "You hurt my grandmother." It wasn't a question.

"By the way, my name is Julie, not Joanne. And that old bat? She had guts, I'll give her that, but Walter was able to handle her."

Abby saw red and flew at Julie with hands raised and claws extended. She tackled her and they both went sprawling onto the filthy floor. Abby got in a few licks before one of the brutes standing outside the room lifted her off the woman. She struggled, but he had an iron grip.

Julie rolled over and wiped blood off her face. Abby was glad to see a long scratch marring that beautiful, deceitful, murdering face.

Walter helped Julie to her feet and she whipped the gun from his hand. Her face twisted in fury as she pointed the weapon at Abby. "I'll kill you for that," she screeched, but Walter ripped the gun from her hands. She tried to grab it back, but he pushed her away.

"We stick to the plan. It has to look like an accident."

Shoving her hair back, Julie smoothed the lines in her face. "It's too late for that, dear, stupid brother. After everything that's happened, the cops know who we are now."

"True, but the police have no proof that we killed them. We need to do it somewhere else. A place that's not connected to us. So what if we joined a choir in Blessing, Texas. That doesn't prove we killed them."

She sneered at her cousin. "Maybe you have a few brain cells after all. Fine. Let's get on with it. The sooner these two are dead the better."

TWENTY-THREE

Fear and a sense of urgency made Noah want to storm the warehouse. There was a car parked in front of the building, and Noah's gut told him they were inside.

His heart raced at the idea of Julie and Walter Camdon killing Abby, but Alex's words of wisdom and caution prevailed.

They had called in backup and the building was surrounded by hidden FBI agents. Noah was crouched behind a large bush near the front door, Bates at his side. He gave a thumbs-up to Alex. Lincoln Camdon was to make a call to Julie and request an emergency meeting. Hopefully it would bring them out of the building.

Alex returned a thumbs-up from where he was hiding in the tree line. The call had been made and the die was cast. *God, please let Abby be alive.*

The door creaked open. Julie Camdon strolled out first and glanced over her shoulder. "Let's move it. I want to get this over with."

Bates stood up on all fours, the fur raised on the back of his neck. Noah grabbed his collar. "Hold, boy." Everything had to be timed perfectly. Noah waited until everyone was out and the door closed behind them. Julie and Walter Camdon had two thugs in tow. The one bringing up the rear had a strong hold on Abby's arm. She was struggling and it infuriated him.

But she was alive! Abby was still alive!

He released the dog's collar. No command was necessary. The dog silently circled around to the back of the group as they stepped out of the building, then Bates lunged and sank his teeth into the guy's arm. Abby stumbled free and fell to the pavement. Noah burst from the shrubbery and yelled, "Drop your weapons."

The other thug dropped his gun as soon as he turned and saw his partner writhing on the ground, suffering Bates's attention.

Weapons drawn, FBI agents surrounded the group.

Everyone threw their hands in the air except for one. Julie Camdon casually reached into her purse, pulled out a gun, whipped around and pointed it at Abby.

Abby was on her knees, trying to push herself off the ground. He'd never get to her in time. He watched, as if in slow motion, the gun rise into the air. Julie's finger pressed the trigger.

"No!" he yelled and took a giant leap forward, but he was too late. Something flew past him and the sound of a shot rang in his ears. Time was suspended as he hit the ground and rolled to his feet. His heart in his throat, Noah raced toward Abby, who was curled up in a ball on the ground. He wrapped his arms around her and his voice shook. "Abby, are you okay? Talk to me. Say something, please."

The chaos around him faded into the background as she uncurled her body and looked up at him. Tears filled her eyes and she clasped the front of his shirt.

"I—I'm okay." After a second, she pulled back and twisted her head around in a frantic motion. "Sam! Where's Sam?"

"I'm right here, brave sister of mine." Sam squatted down close to them. "I'd never have believed it if I hadn't seen it with my own two eyes. The old man had a heart after all."

Abby grabbed his hand and squeezed. "I'm so glad you're okay. I just found you, and now we have a lifetime to get to know one another. What do you mean the old man had a heart after all?"

Sam moved to the side and Noah saw Lincoln Camdon lying a few feet away. He had insisted on accompanying them to the warehouse. The ambulance attendants had arrived and were working hard to revive him. He'd been the blur Noah had seen right before he jumped forward. The old man had taken a bullet for Abby.

Noah kissed Abby on the forehead. "It's your grandfather, sweetheart. He saved your life."

Tears flowed freely down her cheeks and Noah wanted to sweep her away from this horror.

"My grandfather?" she whispered.

Sam grimaced. "Julie's dead. One of the agents shot her at the same time she fired on Abby."

Abby tried to regain her feet and Noah helped her up. "Noah, I have to see him. My grandfather. I have to talk to him."

He wanted to wrap Abby in his arms and take her away from this nightmare, but the pleading look in her eyes had him moving her forward. He shoved through the attendants working on Camdon and took a step back as she knelt by the old man's side and lifted his hand.

Several minutes later, Camdon was pronounced dead and Abby got to her feet. She moved into Noah's open arms and hugged him tight. Pulling back, she peered into his eyes. "I thanked him for saving my life, and told him how to get to heaven, that there was still time, if he wanted to. I know the whole story now. He treated my parents abominably, but he didn't hurt Grammy. Julie and Walter did that." She glanced at the covered gurney that was carrying Julie away. "She hurt my grandmother, and I'll have to work on forgiving her, but now she'll never have a chance to ask for forgiveness."

Noah's heart melted at her words—the mercy she showed toward others. Lincoln Camdon had told him the whole sorry tale on the way to the warehouse. Noah held Abby in his arms, aching for her loss, but proud of the generosity she had shown others. This woman was meant for him and he sensed God's blessing.

"Abby." She looked into his eyes. "I'm in love with you, for as long as God allows us to be together. Please say you'll marry me."

"Noah—"

He placed a finger on her lips. She tried to speak again and he hushed her. "I love you with all my heart and I know Dylan will love you, too."

"Noah—"

"Don't say anything now. Just think about—"

Grabbing him by his shirtfront, she kissed him smack on the lips, pulled back and grinned. "If you'd let me get a word in edgewise, I'd give you my answer. I love you, too. With all of my heart. And the answer is yes. Yes! Yes!"

Noah picked her up and whirled her around, his heart filled with joy. God really did have a knack for bringing good things out of ashes.

EPILOGUE

Six months later

Abby placed a hand over the butterflies in her stomach and smiled nervously at the five most important people in her life and Bates. They stood outside the huge doors guarding the inner sanctum of Camdon International. They were on the top floor of a thirty-story building located in the heart of New York City.

"Do I look okay?"

A lot had happened over the last six months. Her grandfather and Julie were dead, and Walter Camdon would spend a long time in jail. She visited him every week, trying to help in any way she could. He still hated her, but she prayed for him daily. Noah and his father were finally communicating, and he had allowed his dad to visit Dylan. He also promised to get in touch with his half sisters.

When the FBI interrogated Walter, he admitted that he thought the truth was so buried it would never come to light, even though he'd left the three pictures that could possibly lead to his family, to throw everyone off the scent and provide a distraction from their real purpose, which was to remove Abby so they could inherit the Camdon fortune. Walter admitted that they thought Sam was dead, and found out about Abby when they bribed someone to get a copy of the will. They discovered that Abby was next in line to inherit before Julie and Walter.

Noah gave her a peck on the cheek. "Don't forget, deep down, buried under all that Southern charm, lives a steel magnolia, Mrs. Galloway."

The butterflies settled down. "I love hearing you call me that—not," she added, "a steel magnolia, but your wife."

Abby reached over and hugged her grandmother. "Thank you for coming, and thank you for moving to Blessing."

Grammy hugged her back and swiped a tear from her cheek. "I'm just glad to be alive and kicking 'cause I got a new grandson and great-grandson to pester."

Abby squatted in front of Dylan and gave him a hug. He hugged her fiercely, then ducked his head in embarrassment. "I love you, Dylan."

"I love you, too. Mom," he added while studying his feet.

Her heart filled to bursting with happiness and love, Abby held out a hand and her brother took it. "You ready to face the wolves?"

His lips curled in a grin. "You take the lead."

After touring the numerous personal and corporate holdings, Abby and Sam had decided to sell off the posh, expensive houses, cars, etcetera, and had agreed that Sam would handle the business. Abby already had several important jobs: wife, mother, choir director and piano teacher. She and Noah, along with Dylan and Grammy, would reside in Blessing. Sam would visit often.

Gripping the door handle, Abby realized everything had come full circle. She whispered, "Mom, Dad, I hope you're watching. I love you."

She and her brother opened the imposing double doors simultaneously. Abby marched to the head of the long, intimidating table, Sam at her side. She stifled a laugh as the overpaid department heads of the massive corporation stiffened in their seats when Bates circled the table and got a good sniff of each person. With all eyes on her, she gave the room of well-tailored suits her sweetest smile, then released the steel magnolia.

"Good morning, ladies and gentlemen. There's going to be a few changes now that my brother and I are in charge of Camdon International…"

After the meeting, Abby melted into Noah's arms.

"We were listening at the door. You and Sam did great in there."

Abby smiled when Bates let out a happy bark and Dylan laughed, then she stared deeply into Noah's eyes. "I'm glad Sam is handling the company. Did you know they have interests in everything from vacuum cleaners to technology? My grandfather had his hands in many pies. What's it called? Diversification. Noah, we have to get back to Blessing."

He kissed her forehead. "What's the hurry? We could spend a few days in New York, go out to dinner and relax for a change."

She grinned. "I have a church to rebuild and a new piano to buy."

He kissed her on the lips, right there in front of everyone, before turning her loose and facing their small group. "Okay, people, time to go home."

She waved goodbye to Sam and he disappeared back inside the conference room. She turned, took a deep breath, grinned and followed her new family down the hall and out of the building, her heart bursting with love and excitement for their new lifelong journey together.

* * * * *

If you enjoyed this book, pick up these other exciting stories from Love Inspired Suspense.

TRACKER by Lenora Worth
POINT BLANK by Sandra Robbins
THE AMISH WITNESS by Diane Burke
REUNITED BY DANGER by Carol J. Post
TAKEN HOSTAGE by Jordyn Redwood

Find more great reads at www.LoveInspired.com

Dear Reader,

The inspiration for this book came from my very own choir director. She is also a piano teacher, and I often marvel at the talent it takes to play the piano and teach voice lessons. I enjoyed creating a strong but soft woman. Southern women love hair, makeup and clothes, but have also been known to dig a fence-post hole or two. And, of course, my hero is thrown off balance when faced with such a contradictory lady. I hope you enjoy reading about Abby and Noah's adventures as much as I enjoyed writing them.

Liz Shoaf

Get 2 Free Books,
Plus 2 Free Gifts—
just for trying the Reader Service!

YES! Please send me 2 FREE Love Inspired® Suspense novels and my 2 FREE mystery gifts (gifts are worth about $10 retail). After receiving them, if I don't wish to receive any more books, I can return the shipping statement marked "cancel." If I don't cancel, I will receive 4 brand-new novels every month and be billed just $5.24 each for the regular-print edition or $5.74 each for the larger-print edition in the U.S., or $5.74 each for the regular-print edition or $6.24 each for the larger-print edition in Canada. That's a savings of at least 13% off the cover price. It's quite a bargain! Shipping and handling is just 50¢ per book in the U.S. and 75¢ per book in Canada.* I understand that accepting the 2 free books and gifts places me under no obligation to buy anything. I can always return a shipment and cancel at any time. The free books and gifts are mine to keep no matter what I decide.

Please check one: ☐ Love Inspired Suspense Regular-Print   ☐ Love Inspired Suspense Larger-Print
                              (153/353 IDN·GLW2)   (107/307 IDN GLW2)

Name   (PLEASE PRINT)

Address   Apt. #

City   State/Prov.   Zip/Postal Code

Signature (if under 18, a parent or guardian must sign)

Mail to the **Reader Service:**
IN U.S.A.: P.O. Box 1341, Buffalo, NY 14240-8531
IN CANADA: P.O. Box 603, Fort Erie, Ontario L2A 5X3

Want to try two free books from another line?
Call 1-800-873-8635 or visit www.ReaderService.com.

* Terms and prices subject to change without notice. Prices do not include applicable taxes. Sales tax applicable in N.Y. Canadian residents will be charged applicable taxes. Offer not valid in Quebec. This offer is limited to one order per household. Books received may not be as shown. Not valid for current subscribers to Love Inspired Suspense books. All orders subject to approval. Credit or debit balances in a customer's account(s) may be offset by any other outstanding balance owed by or to the customer. Please allow 4 to 6 weeks for delivery. Offer available while quantities last.

Your Privacy—The Reader Service is committed to protecting your privacy. Our Privacy Policy is available online at www.ReaderService.com or upon request from the Reader Service.

We make a portion of our mailing list available to reputable third parties that offer products we believe may interest you. If you prefer that we not exchange your name with third parties, or if you wish to clarify or modify your communication preferences, please visit us at www.ReaderService.com/consumerschoice or write to us at Reader Service Preference Service, P.O. Box 9062, Buffalo, NY 14240-9062. Include your complete name and address.

LIS17R2

SPECIAL EXCERPT FROM

Love Inspired
SUSPENSE

*While Texas Ranger Austin Rivers and border patrol
agent Kylie Perry work together to bring down a drug
cartel, someone's determined to kill Kylie and her newly
adopted baby, Mercedes. Now Kylie and Austin must
shift their focus to uncover why she's being targeted—
before it's too late.*

Read on for a sneak preview of
Sharon Dunn's THANKSGIVING PROTECTOR,
the exciting beginning of the new miniseries
TEXAS RANGER HOLIDAYS,
available October 2017 from Love Inspired Suspense!

Austin stepped closer to her. "I think this is personal,
Kylie. Someone wants you dead."

Mercedes stopped crying. Her soft fingers brushed over
Kylie's neck as she grabbed her collar to hold on to. While
a thousand conflicting emotions tumbled through Kylie's
mind, the only clear thought was that she wanted to keep
Mercedes safe. Mercedes stuck two fingers in her mouth
and stared up at Kylie, a look of total trust in her eyes.

"I think you need to put that kid in protective custody so
you can do your job and resolve this threat," Austin said.

Kylie couldn't believe what she was hearing. "So I can
do my job?" Was that what mattered the most to him?

Austin paced. His hand gestures indicated he was rattled. "Both of you could have died out there." What was going on with him, anyway? He was Mr. Cool Under Fire. She'd never seen him this upset.

"I know that. Don't you think I know that?" Kylie wrestled with even more doubt. More than anything she wanted to keep Mercedes safe, but the thought of being separated from her nearly broke her in half. She was the one who could best protect her, and the shots had been fired at her, not at the baby. Was the little girl really in danger if she stayed? Mercedes had lost her mother. Turning her over to strangers would only add trauma on trauma. Her insides twisted from the turmoil she felt. Austin was right, though—something bad could have happened to Mercedes.

He combed his fingers through his dark blond hair. "We need to get Garcia, and we need to get whoever shot at you. Chances are, they're connected."

"We?" Her jaw tightened. It was clear he was uncomfortable with her new status as a single mother. He just wanted her to be Kylie, unattached, trusted border patrol agent, focused on nothing more than the job. But that wasn't her anymore. She was a mother now. Didn't he understand that?

Don't miss
THANKSGIVING PROTECTOR by Sharon Dunn,
available October 2017 wherever
Love Inspired® Suspense books and ebooks are sold.

www.LoveInspired.com

*When an accident strands pregnant widow Willa Chase
and her twins at the home of John Miller, she doesn't
know if she'll make it back to her Amish community for
Christmas. But the reclusive widower soon finds himself
hoping for a second chance at family.*

Read on for a sneak peek of
AMISH CHRISTMAS TWINS by USA TODAY
bestselling author Patricia Davids,
the first in the three-book **CHRISTMAS TWINS** *series.*

John waited beside Samuel's sleigh and tried
unsuccessfully to curb his excitement. He was almost as
giddy as Megan and Lucy. A sleigh ride with Willa at his
side was his idea of the perfect winter evening, especially
since he didn't have to drive. Lucy was the first one out of
the house. She quickly claimed her spot in the front seat
beside Samuel. Megan came out next and scrambled up
beside her sister. He'd never seen the twins so delighted.

Willa took John's hand as he helped her in. He gave
her gloved fingers a quick squeeze and saw her smile
before she looked down.

Samuel slapped the lines and the big horse took off
down the snow-covered lane. Sleigh bells jingled merrily
in time with the horse's footfalls, and Megan and Lucy
tried to catch snowflakes on their tongues between
giggles.

John leaned down to see Willa's face. "Are you warm

LIEXP0917

enough?" She nodded, but her cheeks looked rosy and cold. John took off his woolen scarf and wrapped it around her head to cover her mouth and nose.

"Danki," she murmured.

"Don't mention it. In spite of the cold, it's a lovely evening to go caroling, isn't it?" The thick snow obscured the horizon and made it feel as if they were riding inside a glass snow globe. The fields lay hidden under a thick blanket of white. A hushed stillness filled the air, broken only by the jingle of the harness bells and the muffled thudding of the horse's feet.

Their first destination was only a mile from John's house. As Lucy and Megan scrambled down from the sleigh, John offered Willa his hand to help her out.

"Was this what you imagined Christmas would be like when you decided to return to your Amish family?"

She shook her head. "I never imagined anything like this. Do you do it every year?"

"We do."

"You aren't going to actually sing, are you, John?"

He threw back his head and laughed. *"Nee*, but I will hum along."

"Softly, dear, softly," she suggested.

He wondered if she realized that she had called him "dear." It was turning out to be an even more wonderful night than he had hoped for.

Don't miss
AMISH CHRISTMAS TWINS
by Patricia Davids, available October 2017 wherever
Love Inspired® books and ebooks are sold.

www.LoveInspired.com